The time to make friends is before you need them.

—An Amish Proverb

Sugarcreek Amish Mysteries

Blessings in Disguise
Where Hope Dwells
The Buggy before the Horse
A Season of Secrets
O Little Town of Sugarcreek
Off the Beaten Path

OFF THE
Beaten Path

ANNALISA DAUGHETY

Guideposts
New York

Sugarcreek Amish Mysteries is a trademark of Guideposts.

Published by Guideposts Books & Inspirational Media
110 William Street
New York, NY 10038
Guideposts.org

Copyright © 2015 by Guideposts. All rights reserved.

This book, or parts thereof, may not be reproduced, stored in a retrieval system, or transmitted in any form or by any means, electronic, mechanical, photocopying, recording, or otherwise, without the written permission of the publisher.

This is a work of fiction. Sugarcreek, Ohio, actually exists and some characters are based on actual business owners or residents whose identities have been fictionalized to protect their privacy. All other names, characters, businesses, and events are the creation of the authors' imaginations, and any resemblance to actual persons or events is coincidental.

Every attempt has been made to credit the sources of copyrighted material used in this book. If any such acknowledgment has been inadvertently omitted or miscredited, receipt of such information would be appreciated.

Scripture references are from the following sources: The Holy Bible, King James Version (KJV). The Holy Bible, New International Version (NIV). Copyright © 1973, 1978, 1984, 2011 by Biblica, Inc. Used by permission of Zondervan. All rights reserved worldwide. www.zondervan.com

Cover and interior design by Müllerhaus
Cover illustration by Bill Bruning, represented by Deborah Wolfe, LTD.
Typeset by Aptara, Inc.

Printed and bound in the United States of America
10 9 8 7 6 5 4 3 2 1

I was blessed to be born into a close family and
equally blessed to have married into one.
This book is dedicated with love to my in-laws,
John and Ann Alliston.
Thank you for welcoming me into your family
as one of your own.
I am so blessed by both of you and
couldn't ask for a better family
to be a part of.
Thanks for all you do for me and Johnny,
and thanks for the wonderful examples you are
to your children and grandchildren.

OFF THE
Beaten Path

Chapter One

Cheryl Cooper had always thought of January as the perfect time to try new things. Over the past few years, she'd attempted the usual, like gym memberships, weight loss, and prayer journals. She'd even tried her hand at sewing (terrible) and painting (better, but no one would ever mistake her for van Gogh). This year, though, she felt confident her new venture would be a success.

"Having second thoughts?" Levi Miller asked. "We can still back out if you'd like." The Amish man leaned against the Swiss Miss counter and regarded her with twinkling blue eyes that just matched his button-down shirt. He still had the sleeves rolled up from a day of work on his family farm. Levi had stopped by the Swiss Miss to drop off a few items and to check with Cheryl about the tour they'd planned together.

Cheryl shook her head. "I think a 'Live Like the Amish' weekend will be a huge hit." People were naturally intrigued by a slower-paced way of life and would likely jump at the chance to spend a long weekend on an Amish farm. But she had an occasional niggle of worry. "I'm just wondering if your family is really okay with it." When she'd mentioned the idea to Levi a few weeks ago, she'd been halfway joking. But he'd thought the plan had merit and had discussed it with his family. Today was the day they'd agreed to begin advertising, and Cheryl was having a hard time pressing the Send button on the press release.

Levi nodded. "*Ja*. We are certain. It is only for a short time. I think our agreed upon times are perfect. They will get here on a Thursday before lunch and depart on Monday afternoon. That is not very long in the great scheme of things." He grinned. "Besides, tourists stop in front of our farm and take photos of *Daed* plowing with his team of horses, or of *Maam* hanging our clothes on the clothesline. We may as well teach them to help us with our chores. Maybe then we will not be such a novelty."

Cheryl chuckled. "Good point." She peered at the computer screen and read over the press release one more time. "I'm making sure to point out that the tour will include authentic food. I think that will be a real selling point." She looked up at him. "Especially the fry pies." A local staple, fry pies were half-moon-shaped fried-dough pockets filled with a wide selection of delectable flavors. Cheryl's favorite was pineapple, but strawberry came in a close second.

"Of course. They will be able to sample a different flavor each day if they want to."

Cheryl typed one final sentence and saved the document. She attached it to the e-mail she'd already composed to several travel agents who regularly arranged Amish country tours. "I'm sending the e-mail now. I did a test registration on the Web site earlier and it worked. I've also checked on a few flight prices from different areas of the country. Flights to Canton aren't too expensive right now, so I think that will make it an attractive getaway for many people, especially with the mild winter we're having." Tour goers would arrange for their own transportation to the Canton airport, where they'd be picked up by bus and brought to Sugarcreek.

Cheryl took a deep breath then pressed the key with a flourish. She looked up at Levi.

"No turning back now," he said with a smile. "I will stop by the store tomorrow and see if anyone has registered yet."

Cheryl watched him go. She'd never say it out loud to anyone, but the prospect of seeing Levi again tomorrow made her happy. Perhaps a little happier than it should.

Cheryl had only lived in picturesque Sugarcreek, Ohio, for a few months, but during that time, she'd come to cherish her friendship with Levi. It was a welcome surprise when her aunt Mitzi had contacted her to see if she'd be interested in moving to Sugarcreek and taking over as manager of the Swiss Miss, Aunt Mitzi's thriving gift shop in the heart of Sugarcreek.

At the time, Cheryl had been at a bit of a crossroads, finding herself on the bad end of a failed romance and locked in a corporate job that gave her little joy. Her widowed aunt was finally going to pursue a lifelong dream of mission work, but she needed to leave her store in good hands.

Cheryl had jumped at the chance, but adjusting to the slower-paced lifestyle had been a challenge. There had been times over the months that Cheryl had questioned her decision, but for the most part, she loved her new life in Sugarcreek.

"I'm ready." A stocky woman with an out-of-season suntan put a jar of Naomi Miller's best-selling strawberry jam on the counter with a thud. "This stuff is so good I could eat it right out of the jar." She giggled. "In fact, sometimes I do."

Cheryl rang up the purchase. "It's one of my favorites too. Have you met Naomi Miller, the woman who makes it? She's here frequently. Her daughter works in the store, and Naomi provides several of my most popular goodies. Aside from the jam, she also supplies homemade bread, fudge, and some other seasonal jams and preserves." Naomi and Cheryl had become fast friends, despite their ten-year age difference and the fact that Naomi was Amish. She was also Levi's stepmother.

The woman nodded. "I haven't been introduced, but I've seen her around. She seems like a sweetie." She hoisted her large bag over her shoulder. "My husband and I moved to the area from California about a month ago, and we came in the Swiss Miss for a few souvenirs to send to our family back home. We passed Naomi as she was leaving the store. The girl at the counter told us she was the one who makes the jam." She pushed a strand of bleached-blonde hair from her face. "In fact, I think the girl said she was her daughter. I don't remember her name though."

Cheryl nodded. "Esther. That's Naomi's youngest daughter. She works here many afternoons." Cheryl handed the woman her change and a bag containing the jam.

"I'm Velma, by the way. Velma Jackson. My husband and I are living at the Raber place."

The Raber homestead was between Sugarcreek and Charm. It had been a Christmas tree farm when Cheryl was little, but she'd heard a few years back that it wasn't any longer. "I used to visit there when I was a little girl." Cheryl smiled. "Welcome to Sugarcreek, Velma. I hope you'll stop in again."

"Oh, you betcha. I'll be back." Velma raised the bag and grinned. "I'll need another fix soon. And I'll have to come back when some of Naomi's fudge is in stock. I'll bet it is delicious."

After Velma left, Cheryl busied herself with tidying up the store in preparation for closing. Although since January wasn't exactly a booming month so far, there wasn't all that much tidying to do. She quickly checked her e-mail, pleased to see that there were already some registrants for the Live Like the Amish weekend. Everyone she'd mentioned it to when she and Levi had first cooked up the idea had thought it would be very popular, and it appeared they were right. At this rate, the tour would be full by tomorrow. She could hardly wait to tell Levi.

She glanced at the clock. Almost closing time. She slipped off her apron and put it beneath the counter. Naomi had made aprons for the Swiss Miss employees, and each day when Cheryl put one on, it immediately boosted her mood. The aprons were red with white hearts on the bibs. Almost every single day a customer commented on how cute they were. Cheryl wondered if she should offer some for sale. She made a mental note to discuss it with Naomi. They had the Swiss Miss name and logo stitched on them. It could be good advertising.

Just as she was about to lock up the store for the day, her cell phone rang.

"Could I speak to Cheryl?" a male voice asked.

"Speaking," Cheryl said. She sank on to the stool behind the counter, and her cat, Beau, jumped onto her lap, purring loudly. He knew it was time to go home.

"My name is Blake Daniels. I'm wondering if you could do me a little favor." Something about his tone told Cheryl he was used to getting his way.

"What can I do for you, Mr. Daniels?"

"Blake. Please call me Blake." He chuckled. "Mr. Daniels is my father."

Lame. Cheryl sighed. "What can I help you with, Blake?"

"I live out in LA," he began. "I'm a manager in Hollywood, and I have a special client who would like nothing more than to be a part of your Live Like the Amish weekend coming up."

Cheryl wrinkled her nose. How in the world had some guy from California found out about her tour? "Oh?"

"You may have heard of her." Blake paused. "The name is Lacey Landers."

Cheryl drew a deep breath. She'd just seen a spot on the news that morning about Lacey. The girl was only in her early twenties, yet she'd taken the world by storm with a string of country and pop hits she'd penned herself. Her face was on the cover of every major magazine. She'd done a few TV movies, and Cheryl had read somewhere that Lacey was getting ready for her big-screen debut.

"That's very flattering, Mr. Daniels, but our tour is primarily geared toward an older clientele. I think Lacey would probably feel a little out of place." The idea of Lacey Landers spending a long weekend at the Millers' farm with a bunch of older folks was amusing. Why would she possibly want to come to Amish country?

Blake sighed loudly. "Cheryl, I can't begin to express how important this is to Lacey. She's been under a lot of stress lately, what with the stalker and all. I'm sure you've heard. It's been in all the major news outlets."

Cheryl rolled her eyes. "Yes, I think I did read something about that. But I really don't know that Lacey would enjoy herself on an Amish weekend. It will be mostly retirees participating, and there is going to be a strict no-cell-phone policy to keep things authentic. Not to mention that we've planned to have several people share rooms." There was no way some starlet would want to share a room with a bunch of grannies for a weekend.

"Lacey really, really wants to participate. She is fully aware of the parameters and thinks it would be fun. She's even planning to disguise herself so she'll fit in."

Cheryl sighed. "I don't know..."

"Please, Cheryl." Blake's voice was pleading. "The poor kid really needs a bit of peace and quiet. She's just off her big stadium tour and is getting ready to star in her first feature film. She's actually portraying an Amish woman. So this would really help her out."

"She wouldn't expect any special treatment?"

"Not at all. She would love to spend time away from the paparazzi and have some peace." He cleared his throat. "And did I mention that in addition to the required payment, we'll make a sizable donation to the charity of your choice? I'll even throw in a few front-row-seat concert tickets for the next time she has a show nearby."

The concert tickets didn't interest her much, but a charitable donation? That had some merit. "The charity of my choice?" Aunt Mitzi could benefit. Cheryl might not want to babysit some pop star for a long weekend, but if it meant Aunt Mitzi could further her mission work in New Guinea, Cheryl would do it.

"I knew I could count on you," Blake said with the air of someone who'd just won what he knew should've been a losing battle.

Once the details were worked out, Cheryl hung up and checked her e-mail to see if any other registrations had come through.

"No way," she said to Beau, who was perched on the counter. "Once I add Lacey to this list, we're full." She could hardly believe it.

Maybe her crazy idea wasn't so crazy after all.

Chapter Two

"A pop star?" Naomi Miller asked the following afternoon. She'd brought a fresh batch of preserves to the Swiss Miss, and Cheryl was filling her in on the events of the previous day.

Cheryl nodded. "Yes. Can you believe it? We're not supposed to tell anyone because they don't want the media to know she's here. Plus she'll be in disguise." She shook her head. "Isn't that about the silliest thing you've ever heard?"

Naomi smiled. "Well, she is also an actress, ja? So maybe being disguised is something she finds fun." Her dark brown eyes sparkled.

"I guess. I just hope I haven't added a whole heap of trouble to the weekend." Cheryl shook her head. "And to make it worse, she's getting ready for a role in a movie. She'll be playing an Amish woman."

"You sound as if you disapprove," Naomi observed.

Cheryl shrugged. "I guess I'm just...overprotective now that I live here and know so many wonderful Amish people."

Naomi looked pleased. "There have been movies about us filmed right here in Sugarcreek. I think those involved tried to portray us in a good light. I saw one of the movies, in fact."

"Really?" Cheryl was shocked. She hadn't expected that.

Naomi nodded. "Ja. We watched it over the summer. They showed it outside in the town square. It was fun to see so many local landmarks on the screen." She placed a hand on Cheryl's shoulder. "Don't worry so much about this actress. It will be fine. Perhaps being on the farm for a few days will be good for her. You never know what *Gott* has in store."

It was just like Naomi to see the bright side. That was one of the many things Cheryl admired about her. "Okay. I'm sure you're right. I just keep envisioning some drama queen who only eats tofu and demands a special kind of bottled water."

Naomi burst out laughing. "She's coming to the wrong place if that is what she is looking for. I have just about finished planning the menu, and there isn't any tofu on it. But there is chicken and dressing, roast beef, and lots of pie."

"Pie? I'm invited, right?" Cheryl teased.

A smile spread across Naomi's pretty face. "I thought one of our group activities could be learning some traditional Amish recipes. Are you up for a cooking lesson?"

Cheryl shook her head. "I think I'll leave that to the experts. I'd be glad to sample though." Sugarcreek was a town full of good cooks, and even so, Naomi was legendary. Her meals would rival any chef.

"Speaking of sampling, are you still planning to have dinner with us tonight so we can finalize the activities for the tour?"

"I've been looking forward to it all week," Cheryl said. "In fact, I skipped lunch in preparation."

Naomi chuckled. "Levi requested chicken and dumplings. I believe he said that was your favorite."

Cheryl felt the heat rise to her face. "He's right. It was sweet of him to remember my favorite dish." She and Levi were close to the same age, and he'd been one of the first people she'd met upon taking over the Swiss Miss. Her aunt Mitzi had introduced them one day when he'd brought some of Naomi's fudge to the shop. "Levi had always planned to marry a sweet girl named Emma," Aunt Mitzi had said. "But she ended up marrying his best friend instead." No stranger to heartbreak, Cheryl had felt an immediate kinship with Levi. Over the months since she'd moved to Sugarcreek, they'd become genuine friends. And since they'd been planning the Live Like the Amish weekend, they'd been spending even more time together than normal.

Naomi gathered her basket and headed toward the door. "Have a *goot* afternoon."

"You too," Cheryl called. She turned her attention back to the inventory list she'd been working on.

A few hours later, she turned down the driveway to the Millers' farm. She took her time crossing the covered bridge. She was still new enough to Sugarcreek that she found covered bridges charming. It was all so peaceful. Her life as a banker in Columbus seemed like a different world than the one she lived in now. As soon as Aunt Mitzi had approached her about taking over the shop so she could fulfill her lifelong dream of being a missionary, a definite sense of peace had come over Cheryl. She knew the situation was the answer to prayer, and even though life in Sugarcreek had been an adjustment, the knowledge that she was where God wanted her to be gave her the peace she needed. And giving Aunt Mitzi the freedom to pursue something she'd wanted for so long made it even better.

"Welcome, Cheryl." Seth Miller waved from near the barn. "Do you want to come see the newest additions to our farm?"

She waved a greeting and headed toward the barn. Naomi hadn't mentioned anything new, but she'd been in a hurry today. "Thanks for having me here, Seth," she said once she reached him. "My stomach has been growling in anticipation all day."

Seth chuckled. "Naomi's cooking will do that." The love shone in his eyes. "It's better than any restaurant."

Cheryl nodded in agreement. She'd had the privilege of eating at the Millers' a few times now. It wasn't lost on her how fortunate she was to have friends like them in her life. The Millers were the kind of people who could be counted on to lend a hand during the tough times and to rejoice during the good ones.

"We have two new baby goats in the barn this week," Seth said. He unlatched the barn door and held it open for her. "They are Nigerian Dwarfs and will be a perfect addition to the petting zoo later in the spring."

Cheryl stepped into the barn and let her eyes adjust to the dim light. She looked around. The pungent aroma of hay reminded her of childhood visits to her grandparents' farm in Virginia. "How many animals live in here?"

"Just the petting zoo animals. Our working animals are in another barn closer to the pasture. We have three goats, two sheep, and four rabbits in here right now. I'm planning to retire one of our horses in a few weeks, and he'll be part of this season's zoo as well." Seth knelt down in front of a stall that held two small goats. "Here are our new little guys." He reached out and patted the head of a solid white goat. "They both have blue eyes." He grinned. "If we weren't about to eat, I'd tell you to go inside and rock them."

"Rock them?" Cheryl asked.

Seth let out a chuckle. "They are already spoiled rotten. Esther has been coming out to visit them each day, and she says they like to be rocked and sung to like babies." His eyes twinkled. "I can tell you from firsthand experience, they don't seem to enjoy my songs. When I try it, they bellow as loud as they can, but Esther's singing seems to soothe them."

Cheryl grinned. "I'll have to come back some time and see how they like me."

"I thought I might find you in here," Naomi called from the doorway. "Dinner is almost ready."

Cheryl and Seth followed Naomi to the farmhouse where Levi and Esther were already waiting and ready to eat.

"So what kinds of things do you think we should plan for the group?" Cheryl asked once everyone was seated around the table with full plates.

"Well, if we want to keep things authentic, I guess we'll just show them some of our chores and the way we do certain things. They can pitch in and help as much as they want to," Levi said.

Esther smiled. "Helping to care for the animals is something I think they'd like. And that's something we do each day."

Cheryl nodded. "You're right. I think that would be a perfect activity. I happened to mention the tour in the store earlier while some customers were there. They were asking what kinds of things the group would do, and I mentioned that caring for the farm animals would probably be part of it."

"Ja. Getting all of them fed and watered, especially in the winter, can be tough," Seth said. "We're blessed because this is a mild winter, but sometimes when the water is frozen solid and the ground is hard, it can be more challenging." He smiled. "But there will be a lot of hay to put out."

"Some of the guests might enjoy a little quilting lesson," Naomi suggested. "Not all of them will, of course, but that's something we could at least talk about."

"And cooking. Don't forget that." Cheryl grinned. "And don't forget my offer to sample the goods."

Naomi chuckled. "Of course." She handed a bowl of potatoes to Seth then turned her attention back to Cheryl. "There are other things like laundry that we do regularly. Some of that might depend on the weather though," Naomi said.

"That all sounds just lovely." Cheryl enjoyed seeing their plans take shape. And ever since they'd started discussing the Live Like the Amish weekend, everything had just fallen into place. "I'll send the entire group an e-mail next Monday with some last-minute suggestions and to make sure no one has any special medical or dietary needs."

"I told you there was no need to worry," Levi said later that night as Cheryl gathered her things to head home. "We've thought through the whole thing. The group will have a wonderful time, and we may have discovered a new business venture."

She nodded. "I'm beginning to think you're right. The remaining piece of the puzzle came together this afternoon just before I drove over here."

"What was that?"

"I can actually thank Naomi. Do you know Mickey Simmons? He's a bus driver. He does bus tours of the area. He even owns his own bus. It's a fancy one too, like bands tour in."

Levi nodded. "I've met him before. He did some work with Daed for a while. He's a nice man."

"He stopped by the store this morning and was asking about the tour. When he heard about it, he thought it sounded like a fabulous idea. He especially thought the group would enjoy working with the animals and doing some of the day-to-day chores that are needed on a farm." Cheryl sure hoped he was right and the group didn't end up feeling like hired help. "He asked if we had someone already contracted to pick the group up from the Canton airport and drive them around because if not he wanted to take part."

"Didn't you already have someone in mind?" Levi asked. They'd discussed that very item last week, and Cheryl had mentioned a few drivers.

"I hadn't asked anyone yet. As soon as Mickey mentioned it, I could tell Naomi thought it was a good idea."

"She has a soft spot for him," Levi said. "Didn't he lose his wife last year?"

Cheryl hadn't lived in Sugarcreek then, but Naomi had filled her in. "Yes. She had cancer. I think Mickey has had a hard time adjusting to life without her." Stories like that always made her sad. "Naomi thought being part of the tour would be good for him." Cheryl smiled. "And I think she also wanted to make sure he had a few home-cooked meals." Although Mickey wouldn't stay at the farm with the group, he'd be around in case they needed to go anywhere. Naomi had been sure to invite him to join the group for meals.

Levi returned her smile. "That sounds about right."

As Cheryl headed home, she ran over all the tour details in her mind. The activities were pretty well planned, the itinerary was done, and Mickey agreeing to serve as the driver was really the last thing on her list.

There was nothing left to do now but wait for the tour group to arrive.

It was going to be a long two weeks.

Chapter Three

Cheryl had never been more thankful for Esther Miller's help. "You're a lifesaver for me today, you know it?"

The girl smiled and put her Swiss Miss apron over her dress. With her clear skin, rosy cheeks, and small features, she looked just like one of the fresh-faced Amish girls on the cover of many popular books. "*Danki.*"

"I can't believe tomorrow is the big day," Cheryl said as they worked together to tidy up the front of the store. "I sure hope everything goes well."

"You and Levi have planned the weekend very well," Esther said. "And Maam is ready with some of her best recipes and plenty of activities that will give them a taste of our life here in Sugarcreek." She grinned. "I think it will be lots of fun."

Cheryl hoped Esther was right. She'd spent the last week making last-minute arrangements and getting all of the various travel information from each of the tour attendees. She needed to know if a flight was late or if someone missed a leg of their journey to Sugarcreek so that she could let Mickey know to wait a little longer at the airport. "I think we've thought of every possible problem that could arise, so maybe we're prepared." She and Levi had gone over some worst-case-scenario situations yesterday so they'd have a plan in place. If someone got sick, she would drive them to the nearby urgent care or emergency room, depending on the situation. If someone had a family emergency, she or Mickey would drive them back to the airport. If someone didn't enjoy authentic Amish food, she would bring pizza. Although the idea that one of the guests wouldn't enjoy Naomi's cooking was so far-fetched, she and Levi had both laughed at the thought.

She felt very prepared. "I am just ready to get the weekend started." This would be the first big new venture she'd started since taking over the Swiss Miss, and she wanted it to go well. The biggest question mark in her mind was how Lacey Landers would fit in. She'd seen yet another story in the headlines yesterday that claimed Lacey was being stalked and was fearful for her life.

The bell above the door jingled, and a red-faced man stormed inside. "I'd like to speak to the manager," he spewed. "Her name is Cheryl something or other, and she's not from these parts. Mitzi never would've let this happen."

Cheryl met Esther's wide-eyed stare and motioned for her to follow her. The two of them scurried behind the counter. Cheryl wanted some distance between them and the angry man. "I'm Cheryl Cooper," she said, trying to keep her voice calm. "Is there something I can help you with?" From the glowering expression on his face, it was clear he wasn't there for the strawberry jam.

"Yes." He stomped down the aisle toward her and slammed a piece of paper on the counter. "You can explain *this*."

She peered at the Live Like the Amish weekend flier that he'd put on the counter. "What would you like to know? I'm sorry to tell you that the tour is all booked up." She tried to sound calm, but her shaky voice told another tale.

"How dare you offer this tour?" His voice shook with rage. "This is something I've planned to do for a long time. I was just about to finally get all my ducks in a row and have an Amish family onboard." He pounded his fist on the counter. "And then I see that *you* beat me to it."

Cheryl stared, stunned. She'd never even seen this man before in her life. "I'm so sorry, sir. But I don't guess I know what you mean. I certainly didn't steal your idea. The Millers and I came up with this all on our own, and the tour will be visiting their farm." She motioned toward Esther. "The whole family is really going out of their way to be hospitable and give the group a glimpse into the Amish way of life."

The man's red face twisted into an ugly sneer. "Well, isn't that just the most special thing I've ever heard? I'm so glad things are going so well for you and your little tour."

Cheryl shook her head. "I'm very sorry you are so upset. Do you mind at least telling me your name?" The old adage told her to keep her friends close and her enemies closer. In this case, she'd at least like to know her enemy's name.

"Richard Wellaby. And you haven't heard the last of me." He turned on his heel and stomped out as quickly as he'd entered, grumbling under his breath.

Cheryl let out a breath. "Well that was odd." She watched through the window as Richard stormed down the sidewalk. "And kind of scary."

"Ja." Esther nodded in agreement. "He is not a nice man. And I was also a little afraid he might have a heart attack or something."

The bell above the door jingled and Cheryl looked up, half expecting Richard to barge in again. Much to her relief, it was Kathy Snyder from the Honey Bee Café, one of Cheryl's favorite nearby lunch stops.

"How are you ladies today?" Kathy asked as she approached the counter. "Although maybe I don't even have to ask that. I ran into Mean Richard on the way in, and he was all worked up about something. I hope he wasn't rustling up trouble."

"Mean Richard?"

"Mean as a snake. He used to own a gift shop just down the street, but he closed it a few years back. He likes to keep things stirred up around here though." She smiled. "Your aunt Mitzi can tell you about the time he accused her of selling Naomi's fudge at a discount just to undercut his business." Kathy let out a chuckle. "Of course, nothing could've been further from the truth. I think Richard just wakes up on the wrong side of the bed every day."

"I've never met him until today," Cheryl said. "But I guess I won't forget him now. He was pretty upset with me." She quickly filled Kathy in on the exchange that had taken place. "I certainly didn't steal his idea. I don't even know him."

Kathy nodded. "He operates a few Amish country tours on the side now. I'm not sure if he drives them or hires a driver, but I doubt he gets many repeat customers. Let's just say there are some people who aren't really cut out for working with the public."

"And I'd say he's one of them," Cheryl said. She turned to Esther. "Can you go finish stocking the shelf of Amish dolls? I want that full before tomorrow."

Esther nodded. "Ja."

Kathy motioned toward the office. "Mind if we have a chat in private? I need your help."

"Sure."

Once they were in the office, Kathy took a deep breath. "I am very likely overstepping my boundaries here, so feel free to tell me to mind my own business."

Cheryl grinned. "I haven't even heard what you need help with yet, and I can already tell you that you shouldn't worry."

"You've met the girl who works for me named Heather, right?" Kathy asked. "She's very quiet, hardly says a word. She's such a sweet girl and a hard worker."

Cheryl nodded. "Sure. She makes the best mochas and always blushes when I say so."

"That's her." Kathy sighed. "I know this will sound a little nuts, but I'm worried about her."

"How so?" It was just like Kathy to be concerned about one of her employees. Her big heart was one of the reasons they'd become friends. In fact, she'd just told Cheryl last week that she was going to be donating the day-old bread and such from the café to the local food bank and had even invited Cheryl to pitch in some afternoon soon to help serve those in need of a meal.

"Heather is in her freshman year of college, but she hasn't dated much, if at all. And suddenly today there's this guy in the café who is paying all kinds of attention to her." She shook her head. "There's something about him that I just don't trust."

"What does Heather say?"

Kathy smiled. "Not much. But she fell for every line he tried, and I know she made plans to see him tomorrow. I know I should just stay out of it, but I can't help but worry."

"Is he from around here?"

She shook her head. "I don't guess so. He told her he was staying at a local hotel, but he'd be in town for a while."

"How can I help?" Cheryl wasn't sure what Kathy wanted her to do. It wasn't like she and Heather were anything more than acquaintances. They saw each other most mornings when Cheryl grabbed her morning coffee, and lots of times they bumped into each other at church on Sundays, but they weren't close friends. Certainly not "get involved in each other's personal lives" kinds of friends.

"Well, everyone knows you're pretty good at getting to the bottom of things."

Cheryl laughed. "Is that a polite way of saying that I'm nosy?"

"No! That's not what I mean at all. I just meant that over the past few months, you've helped the local police solve some pretty interesting cases. So it stands to reason that maybe you're the best person I know to find out what this guy is really up to." Kathy shrugged. "I just want to know if he's okay or if he's up to no good."

Kathy's words rang true. In the months since Cheryl had arrived in Sugarcreek, she'd been instrumental in helping to solve some local mysteries. It hadn't been her intention, but things had just worked out that way. "Well, thanks for the vote of confidence." She thought for a moment. Heather did seem like a sweet girl. She hated for her to get hurt by some guy who was just passing through town and feeding her a line. "I'll help however I can."

"Perfect." Kathy grinned. "I was hoping you'd say that. I overheard him say that he'd be in tomorrow for an early lunch. Maybe you can swing by before the tour group arrives and see if you can find out any dirt."

"Sounds like a plan." Cheryl said good-bye to Kathy then hurried to help Esther close up the store. Between investigating a potentially rogue Romeo and greeting a busload full of people, tomorrow would be a busy day.

Chapter Four

The buzzing cell phone brought Cheryl from a deep sleep. She managed to open one eye and glance at the clock. It was still an hour before her alarm would go off. Who could be texting her at this hour?

She reached out her hand and felt around on the nightstand until she made contact with the phone. Through bleary eyes, she read the screen.

> Lacey is en route. Make sure no one in town knows and no one alerts the media. Already having issues with someone speculating she is headed to Ohio. Trying to find the leak now. Make sure it isn't on your end.

Nothing like a totally offensive text to wake her up. Cheryl sat up and frowned at the screen as she reread Blake's message. As if she would go around telling everyone in town that Lacey would be on the tour. She'd only told Naomi and Levi, and she knew neither of them had alerted any media. Nor would they. Because they, like Cheryl, didn't care if Lacey was famous or not. They only cared if she had a nice time on the tour.

She wrote and deleted three snippy messages before settling on one. *No need to worry. No leak here. Thanks for the heads-up.* She should totally get some kind of prize for being so polite.

Now that sleep was out of the question, Cheryl decided to get ready for the day. She took greater care than normal as she did her makeup and hair. Her red hair always had a tendency for being unruly, so any day she had extra time to spend taming it was welcome.

The upside to her early morning wake-up call was that she'd have time to stop by the Honey Bee for breakfast before opening the store. She was pretty sure Naomi had once shared an Amish proverb about making the most of one's time, and that was what she intended to do.

Kathy Snyder greeted her as soon as she walked in the door. "I'm so glad to see you here so early," she said. "I was expecting you for lunch, but this is even better."

Cheryl never got tired of walking into the Honey Bee. The bistro atmosphere was warm and welcoming. The smells coming from the kitchen always made her stomach growl, and she adored the cute decorations—especially the zooming trail of a honeybee that was painted on the floor from the counter to the seating area. "I happened to be up a little earlier than normal today, so I thought a Belgian waffle was just what my day needed to start off on the right track."

Kathy grinned. "That's right. It is a big day for you. I'm sure it will all go smoothly. We're looking forward to greeting your guests for coffee later this afternoon before they head to Naomi's." She motioned toward Heather, who stood waiting at the cash register with a dreamy expression on her face. "Heather will ring you up, and I'll let them know in the kitchen that you need a waffle plate." She paused for a moment before heading to the kitchen. "You're not the first person in the café today though—someone else beat you here," she said pointedly. "Although I'm pretty sure he came in for more than just waffles," she said in a low voice with a glance at Heather.

Heather giggled, the pleased look unmistakable.

Kathy sent a pleading look in Cheryl's direction before disappearing into the kitchen.

So the mystery man was here? Perfect. Now Cheryl could combine a little sleuthing with her breakfast. Not a bad way to start the day. Plus, now she'd be able to spend her entire lunch break at the Swiss Miss preparing for guests instead of at the Honey Bee playing detective. And to think, it was all thanks to Lacey Lambert's overprotective manager and his early morning text.

"Kathy is just saying that," Heather said as she rang up Cheryl's order. Her broad smile gave her away though. She definitely thought the mystery guy was interested in more than waffles.

"I see a sparkle in your eyes," Cheryl said. "Is this guy someone special?"

Heather shrugged as she handed Cheryl the receipt. "We only just met so I guess it's too soon to tell." She beamed. "But I hope so."

Cheryl nonchalantly peered into the seating area. She could see a blond guy alone at a table, sipping a cup of coffee and using an iPad. "I don't recognize him. Is he from around here?"

"Oh no. He's not. He says he'll be around for a few weeks though." Heather looked up as another customer entered the café.

Cheryl waved good-bye as Heather greeted the other customer. She entered the seating area and took a seat that allowed her to face the guy in question. She observed him for a moment. He looked out of place. His sun-streaked hair and tanned face might be customary on a surfboard, but in sleepy Sugarcreek, Ohio, in the middle of January? He stuck out like a sore thumb.

She let her gaze fall to his left hand. No ring and no obvious tan lines where a ring had been. So that was good news. Maybe he was just on vacation. Although a single guy in his twenties wasn't really the typical tourist for Sugarcreek. She had to agree with Kathy's assessment of the situation: something seemed off.

"Here's your coffee," Heather said, approaching her table. "Mocha with just a splash of peppermint."

Cheryl grinned. "Sounds wonderful."

Heather carefully placed the cup on the table. "The waffle will be out any minute." She walked over to the blond guy. "Michael, can I get you anything?"

Cheryl watched their interaction. He sure was laying it on thick. His megawatt smile, complete with dimple, didn't quite reach his eyes though. She strained to hear his low voice.

"So dinner tonight? Someplace local?" he asked. "And I want to see all the sights." He paused. "Of course, you're going to be the prettiest sight I see."

Heather giggled, and Cheryl fought the urge to gag. *At least use a decent line on the poor girl.*

"Of course. I'd be glad to show you around," Heather said. She grimaced as the front door opened. "I have to go take their order."

"Hurry back," he said with a wink as she headed toward the cash register. "I might get lonely."

Cheryl watched her go. The girl was practically walking on air. It was time for a little intervention. She picked up her coffee and walked toward his table. "Michael, is it?" she asked as she approached.

He looked up from his iPad and swiped the screen, but not before she could see that he was reading *People*. "Yes." He furrowed his brow. "Do I know you?"

She shook her head. "Just consider me part of the Sugarcreek welcome wagon. Unofficially, of course." She smiled. "I manage the Swiss Miss next door. It's a gift shop, in case you're looking for some souvenirs to take back home to your family. Maybe a toy for your kids?"

He burst out laughing. "Sorry, lady. No kids. I do have a niece though." He looked at her suspiciously. "How'd you know my name?"

"Oh, I guess I heard Heather call you by name. I'm Cheryl Cooper." She stuck out her hand, and he shook it.

"Michael Rogers." He took a sip of coffee.

"I do hope you'll stop by the Swiss Miss. We have authentic Amish-made gifts. My suppliers are all from the local area."

He perked up. "Amish, huh? Now *that* I might be interested in."

Before she could question him further, the song playing on the overhead speaker changed. Lacey Landers's latest hit blared.

"Don't you think she's an amazing artist?" Michael asked. "She writes her own stuff and everything."

"I suppose she's quite accomplished for one so young." Even though Cheryl already had Lacey pegged as a diva, she had to admit the girl had talent.

"Twenty-four. Can you imagine? Twenty-four and that successful. Some people have all the luck." Michael frowned. "Anyhow, thanks for letting me know about your store."

Cheryl knew she'd been dismissed, but she continued to stand at the table. She wracked her brain for something else to ask him that might let her know if he was truly up to no good or if Kathy was just being overprotective.

"Can I help you with something else?" He looked puzzled.

"No. It was nice to meet you. Enjoy your stay in Sugarcreek." She headed back to her table. *That* was what she should've tried to find out. Where he was staying. Maybe she could manage to get it out of Heather at lunch.

She sat down to a steaming plate of Belgian waffles and doused them with syrup.

Michael passed by her table without a word. She watched him stop briefly at the counter to speak to Heather. She hadn't been able to get a good read on him. Perhaps he was just in Sugarcreek to get away for a few days. She didn't want to cast him as a villain unless he gave her a reason.

Still though, something about him seemed off.

And once the Live Like the Amish tour was underway, she intended to find out what.

Chapter Five

It was always nice to see the store busy, but it was especially nice on a chilly January day. Although there would be more time for shopping on Monday before the bus headed back to the airport, Cheryl had decided to have the group stop by the Swiss Miss before they went to the farm. And judging by the sales Esther had been ringing up, that had been a great decision.

She watched as an elderly couple wearing matching jogging suits browsed the aisle containing Amish dolls. The woman exclaimed with delight at one of the dolls, and the look her husband gave her was one of such adoration, it brought a tear to Cheryl's eye. Would anyone ever look at her that way again? Most days she was able to let go of the romantic disasters of the past and open herself up to the path God had clearly placed her on. But sometimes...sometimes she wondered if her chance at love had already passed her by.

The jingling bell above the Swiss Miss door brought her out of what might've turned into a pity party. A spry old lady wearing a purple cape and matching hat entered the shop. Her cheeks appeared flushed from the cold, and she hurried toward the counter as fast as her orthopedic shoes would carry her.

Cheryl motioned to Esther that she'd help the woman so Esther could continue ringing up purchases for the line of customers.

"Is everything okay?" Cheryl asked.

The older woman's face was wrinkled, but her eyes were a bright green. She stared at Cheryl for a long minute, fighting to catch her breath.

"Don't worry. You aren't late or anything," Cheryl said. "The whole group is still here. Did you check out some of the shops next door?" Since she'd been the one to plan the itinerary, she'd been sure that Mickey gave the group plenty of time to visit some of the other stores in the vicinity. He'd told them what time to meet back at the Swiss Miss though, and according to the clock on the wall, the woman had only made it back with a minute to spare.

"The whole group?" the woman asked.

Cheryl nodded. "Of course. I can't tell you how happy we all are to have each of you here. The weekend at the Millers' farm is going to be a lot of fun." She smiled as the woman began to relax and breathe more evenly. "When I first started talking to Naomi and Levi about hosting the Live Like the Amish weekend, I wasn't at all sure anyone would be interested." She motioned around the crowded shop. "But clearly there was a lot of interest. In fact, I had to turn people away."

"Is that so?" the woman asked. "I, for one, can't think of anything that sounds better right now than a weekend in Amish country." She managed a shaky smile. "I'm just glad I got here in time."

Before Cheryl could ask her where she was from or her name, Mickey clapped his hands.

"All aboard," he called. "We have three more stops before the farm." He grinned. "And one of them is lunch. You don't want to miss it."

Cheryl waved good-bye to the group as they filed past her. She watched out the window as they climbed on to the tour bus. When the last one had gotten on the bus, she closed the shop door and leaned against it. "Whew."

Esther giggled. "That was the busiest we've been since Christmas." She shook her head. "I told a few of them that I would see them at my house later. I think it confused them that I am not wearing my Amish clothes." Esther was in *rumspringa*, and as such, she was free to wear *Englischer* clothes if she wanted. She switched back and forth between her simple Amish dress and bonnet and jeans, a T-shirt, and tennis shoes. "Oh no," Esther called out. "It looks like someone left a hat behind."

Cheryl made her way to the counter where Esther stood. A purple hat was crumpled in a heap near the cash register. "I know just who that belongs to," Cheryl said. "That sweet lady who ran in just before the bus left. She thought she was going to be late. Bless her heart, she was so flustered she must've forgotten it." Cheryl picked up the hat and smoothed the garment then set it on the counter. "I'll take it to the farm later today. I'm sure she'll be chilly without it. My mom always told me that not having your ears covered is the best way to catch a cold."

The bell over the front door rang. "Did I miss it?" An older woman asked, hurrying inside. "The bus. Did I miss the bus?"

Cheryl nodded. "Yes, ma'am. I'm so sorry."

"My bag was on there," the woman said, clearly irritated. As she came closer, Cheryl couldn't help but widen her eyes. Standing before her was none other than Lacey Landers. In spite of the frumpy clothes and the gray wig, the girl's beauty was still stunning.

"Lacey?" Cheryl whispered.

She nodded then broke into a big smile. "You totally bought me as an old lady at first, right?" she whispered back.

Cheryl nodded. "Yes."

"Awesome."

"So what happened? What caused you to miss the bus?"

The girl sighed. "Did you know the world's largest cuckoo clock is here? That was a photo op I totally couldn't miss." She held up an iPhone and showed Cheryl the image on the screen.

"You missed the bus because you were taking a cuckoo clock selfie." Cheryl had to fight to keep from rolling her eyes.

"Yeah. So I'm going to need you to give me a ride." Lacey smiled, her perfect white teeth gleaming. "Please."

Just like her manager, Lacey seemed like the kind of person who rarely heard the word *no*. "Of course. I need to finish up a few things here, and then I'll be glad to take you." Cheryl raked a hand through her wild red hair. "I wonder why Mickey left without you? He was supposed to count and make sure everyone was present before he left."

Lacey shrugged. "I don't know. But I need my bag." She frowned. "It has everything in it. My makeup. My phone charger. I need it." She held up a small messenger bag. "I have this one, but it doesn't have much in it. My *life* is in that bag."

Cheryl sighed. "We'll get you to the bus just as soon as we can. Let me call Mickey's cell phone to see where they are." She'd planned for the group to visit a bookstore, have a buffet lunch at

Dutch Valley, and then stop by the Honey Bee Café for coffee before the group headed to the Millers' farm. "His phone is going to voice mail." She slipped her phone back in her pocket. "I'll try him again in a minute. Feel free to look around for a bit while I get a few things tied up here."

Lacey shrugged. "Okay." She picked up an Amish doll from a nearby shelf. "Creepy. What's the deal with its face?"

"The Amish don't put faces on their dolls for a couple of reasons, but one big one is to teach children that we're all alike in the eyes of God," Cheryl explained. "No matter our looks or place in society, to God it's what's inside that matters."

Lacey looked thoughtful. "I like that." She smiled. "I like that a lot." She scooped up a handful of the small dolls. "I think I'll get some as gifts."

Wonders never cease. Cheryl had expected the pop star to sneer at the explanation, not embrace it. "Esther can ring you up," she said, motioning toward the register. "Or if you'd rather wait and get them on Monday before the bus takes you back to the airport, you'll be stopping by here again then."

Before Lacey could answer, the door burst open and two burly men ran inside and began searching the store, looking frantically on every aisle.

Lacey dropped the Amish dolls back on the shelf and scurried behind Cheryl.

"Can I help you gentlemen?" Cheryl asked. The men were clearly looking for something.

The taller man stopped looking around and walked to where Cheryl and Lacey stood. "Where is she?" he asked. His tanned skin, dark jacket, and sunglasses reminded Cheryl of a mobster movie she'd seen once.

"Where is who?" Cheryl asked.

Lacey began to slowly make her way to the counter where Esther stood frozen.

"The woman in purple. We know she was here."

Cheryl took a deep breath. What was with this day? "There was a lady on our tour group who was wearing purple, but honestly that's a popular color."

The man nodded. "Sorry to startle you, ma'am." He motioned for his friend to join them. "I'm Detective Riggins, and this is my partner Detective McGraw." He flashed a badge in Cheryl's direction. "FBI."

Detective McGraw sauntered over and stuck out a hand. "Sorry to bother you nice people. I'm McGraw."

Cheryl shook the offered hand. "I guess I don't understand what the fuss is about. Can you start at the beginning?"

The two men looked at each other. Detective Riggins nodded. "The woman who came in here earlier was running from us. She's a wanted criminal."

Cheryl widened her eyes. "That sweet old lady?"

McGraw nodded. "She's not so sweet. In fact, she can be very dangerous. We watched her come inside, but we wanted to let the store clear out some before we came in."

"She got on the tour bus." Cheryl couldn't believe it. She'd practically forced the old lady onto the bus.

"On a bus, huh?" Riggins asked. "Do you know where said bus is now?"

Cheryl nodded. "I do. I'm about to go meet up with them. They only had three stops before they are scheduled to arrive at their final destination, the Millers' farm."

Riggins didn't look pleased. "We're going to need you to take us to them, pronto. But when you get there, don't raise an alarm. We want to take her by surprise so she won't run again."

Cheryl fought the urge to ask what crime the little old lady had committed. Based on how riled up the detectives were, it must've been something pretty bad. "I can do that." She motioned to Lacey. "You ready?"

Lacey nodded. "Yep." She grinned. "Looks like our day just got a lot more exciting."

Cheryl told Esther good-bye and led Lacey and the agents out the door. "At least this explains why Mickey left without you," she said as she and Lacey got in her car. "The count was correct because that lady was in your spot."

Lacey giggled. "Yep. It must've been her lucky day."

Thanks to Lacey's cuckoo clock selfie, there was now a criminal on the Live Like the Amish tour. Lucky day, indeed. Cheryl drove in silence toward the bus's first stop.

At least the day couldn't get any worse.

Chapter Six

Cheryl tossed her cell phone back in her bag. Mickey still wasn't picking up. The previous stops had been a bust, as the tour bus was nowhere in sight. "They must be at lunch," Cheryl explained to Lacey.

"Those men are getting super irritated," Lacey said. "Also, that one with the sunglasses needs some serious waxing. Did you see his unibrow when he took off his glasses?"

Cheryl took a deep breath. "I didn't notice. But for what it's worth, he doesn't seem like the kind of guy who'd willingly get his eyebrows waxed."

Lacey popped her gum. "Whatevs. He should totally get onboard. Most of the men I know don't mind it." She grinned. "My last boyfriend was just as much of a spa junkie as I am."

"I'm sure." Cheryl tightened her grip on the steering wheel as she headed toward the Dutch Valley restaurant. The big buffet was one of Cheryl's favorites, and she knew the tour guests would enjoy it as well.

"Is that your stomach growling?" Lacey giggled. "Does that mean you didn't eat breakfast? You know, that's the most important meal of the day. I always have a smoothie—fresh, of course—and some oatmeal with just a little flaxseed and chia sprinkled on top."

The girl never stopped talking. Since they left the Swiss Miss, Lacey had filled the silence with her commentary on everything from her current favorite gum flavor (watermelon) to her thoughts on the unfairness of not being able to use her phone while on a flight.

"I ate breakfast," Cheryl said calmly. "It's past lunchtime now though, and I guess I'm hungry again." No point in telling Lacey her stomach growled at the thought of hot biscuits and apple butter, a staple at nearly every restaurant in Sugarcreek.

Cheryl pulled into a space near the Dutch Valley entrance. The parking lot was packed, including a couple of tour buses. "Wait here. Let me run in and see if they've arrived yet." She slammed the door before Lacey could comment.

Detectives Riggins and McGraw followed her up the steps to the restaurant. "Have you reached the driver yet?" Riggins asked.

Cheryl shook her head. "Nope. He hasn't picked up. Maybe his phone is dead or something."

Detective McGraw held the door open for Cheryl, taking her by surprise. The men had grown more and more irritated with each stop, so his small act of kindness was a shock.

"Thanks," she said.

He nodded.

"I'm looking for Mickey Simmons," she explained to the Amish woman at the hostess stand. "He was bringing in a tour group today."

The woman shook her head. "That reservation got cancelled."

Cheryl's stomach lurched. "I was the one who made that reservation. Who cancelled it?"

The woman shrugged her shoulders. "I have no idea. There was a note on the stand earlier that said to cancel it. I guess someone called in."

"Can you check to see who took the call?" Detective Riggins asked.

"I have no way of knowing who may have taken the message." She motioned toward the busy cashier's desk. There were four women there selling merchandise, ringing up customers from the restaurant, and handing out brochures to area attractions. "There was a shift change since the message came in. I'm sorry."

Detective Riggins thanked the woman then guided Cheryl to the door. "Any other ideas?" he asked once they were outside. "Do you realize the more time that passes, the worse of a situation this will be?"

His words sent a chill down Cheryl's spine. Was the tour group in trouble? Or was it the detective's job to treat every case like a dangerous situation? "Maybe they went straight to the Millers' farm." She managed a weak smile. "It's very possible that Mickey and Naomi made those plans and just didn't tell me. Knowing Naomi, she probably wanted them to have a home-cooked meal." That must be it, although she wished Levi or Naomi had mentioned it to her this morning. "We were all in such a frenzy this morning, they may have forgotten to tell me that change of plans."

The detectives seemed satisfied. "Lead the way to the farm," Riggins said, his face a mask void of emotion.

"Looks like they skipped out on the lunch stop," Cheryl explained as she got in the car.

Lacey narrowed her eyes. "That's weird. The bus driver guy kept telling us how delicious lunch was going to be. He went on and on and on about some kind of fried pies or something." She sighed. "My phone is nearly dead." She held it up. "I really need my charger from my bag."

Cheryl white knuckled the steering wheel. "We'll be there soon. Just sit back and enjoy the drive." She glanced in her rearview mirror and noted the detectives' dark sedan following behind her. A second unmarked car pulled out directly behind them. "That's odd. I think I noticed that white car at the coffee shop too."

Lacey turned around to see the vehicle in question then slumped down in her seat. "No way."

Cheryl glanced over at Lacey. Her elderly woman makeup was beginning to smear a bit, and her bifocals had been replaced by sunglasses. Probably designer. "What's wrong?"

"That car. You're right. They were at the coffee place. I think I saw that same car behind us at the bookstore too." She slumped farther in the seat. "They're here for me."

"Who is?"

"Paparazzi. I can smell them a mile away. I just thought I was safe here."

"Don't be silly," Cheryl said, trying to keep the uncertainty out of her voice. "I'm sure it's just a coincidence." She slowed down as she approached the Millers' driveway and put on her blinker.

She turned down the driveway followed by the detectives.

Lacey peered over her seat. "See?" she whispered. "They're turning too."

Cheryl furrowed her brow. It did seem odd. "Just stay put when we stop, okay? From outside the car, you look like a sweet old lady." She motioned toward the glasses in Lacey's lap. "Might want to switch those out though."

Lacey nodded. "Will do." She put on the bifocals and slumped down a little more in the seat.

Cheryl got out of the car and joined McGraw and Riggins. "Maybe Naomi has been in touch with Mickey. I'm sure she or Levi will know where the group is." Her words came out quickly, and she remembered the way Lance used to tease her about talking too fast when she got nervous. "Levi has been helping me plan the tour," she said, deliberately slow.

Riggins held up his hand to stop her. "Who are the yahoos in the white car? Locals?" He motioned over his shoulder where the car was parked behind the FBI sedan.

Cheryl shook her head. "I'm not sure." She tried to get a view of the people inside the white vehicle. The guy in the passenger seat slumped down and pulled a hat down low on his head. Whoever he was, he didn't care to be recognized. She sighed. "Look, there's something you need to know about the woman in my car."

McGraw leveled his eyes on her. "Yeah? What's that?"

"Do you know who Lacey Landers is?"

The men exchanged a glance and nodded.

"Of course. Doesn't everyone?" Riggins asked.

"Well that's her in my car. She's in disguise. She was supposed to be on the bus tour, but I guess your suspect took her place."

McGraw let out a snort. "No way. You think she'd give me her autograph? My little girl is a huge fan."

"I don't care if Queen Elizabeth herself is in the car," Riggins said sharply. "I think we all need to focus on the task at hand. Wait here."

Cheryl and McGraw watched in silence as Riggins marched past the vehicles and stopped at the white car. He exchanged what looked like heated words then flashed his badge at the driver. In a matter of seconds, the white car began to back out of the driveway.

"What's going on out here?" Naomi asked from the porch. She stepped off the porch, followed by Levi and her husband, Seth. "Is everything okay, Cheryl? You look worried."

Cheryl introduced the detectives and quickly filled the Millers in on what was going on. She motioned for Lacey to join them, and the girl made her way to where they stood.

"Thank you *soooo* much for sending that car away," Lacey said, taking Riggins by the arm. "I would just as soon no photos show up of me in this getup." She smoothed her paisley printed dress and laughed.

Riggins ignored her and turned his attention to Naomi. "Did you communicate with the bus driver after the bus left the store?"

She shook her head. "No. I was just telling Levi they should've been here by now. I thought they must've taken some extra time at one of their other stops."

"I'm afraid not, ma'am. It looks like something a little more sinister happened."

"So the whole bus is just...gone?" Levi asked.

"It sure appears that way," McGraw agreed.

Cheryl took a deep breath and offered up a silent prayer.

How did a bus full of people disappear in broad daylight?

Chapter Seven

McGraw and Riggins stood to the side, deep in conversation. From their growls and gestures, it appeared they didn't agree on the best course of action.

"They don't seem like they like each other much, do they?" Lacey whispered. "I thought partners were supposed to get along."

Cheryl shrugged. "I guess they're just under a lot of stress." She could relate. She turned to Levi. "What should we do?" His presence had a calming effect on her.

He held her gaze for a moment. "I guess we wait to see what they say. I do not believe there is much we can do right now anyway." He looked from Cheryl to Naomi. "And I hope the two of you will not investigate. It sounds much too dangerous for that."

A small smile played on Naomi's lips. "*Ach*, now, Levi. It is never our intention to get involved. We just try to be helpful."

"That's true. Plus sometimes we just can't help it," Cheryl explained. "Besides, this time there are federal authorities involved. I'm sure they'll locate the bus in no time."

Lacey let out an unladylike snort. "From the looks of them, I wouldn't be so sure." She grabbed Cheryl's arm. "Actually, I wonder if this whole thing isn't my fault."

"The clock selfie?" Cheryl asked. "I don't know if that would've made a difference. Although I suppose that woman wouldn't have been able to get on the bus if you'd been there."

Lacey gave her a look of utter disbelief. "No. I mean I wonder if the bus disappearing was because *I* was supposed to be on it." She wrung her hands. "What if someone totally followed me here? And they hijacked that bus to kidnap me?" Her voice grew louder and shriller with each word. "My manager has received threats, you know. That's part of the reason I'm here in the first place." She fanned herself. "And he texted me this morning to tell me to be on high alert because he thought there was a leak somewhere along the line. If the paparazzi know I'm in Sugarcreek, the guy after me might know too."

Cheryl looked at Lacey in disbelief. Was she so self-centered that she really thought the bus disappearing had something to do with her? "I think you should calm down. I doubt this has anything to do with you."

Lacey narrowed her eyes. "You have no idea what it's like to be me. Always looking over my shoulder. Never sure who you can trust."

The words *drama* and *queen* ran through Cheryl's mind, but she refrained from saying them out loud.

Riggins and McGraw rejoined the circle. "What's the commotion?" Riggins asked, nodding his head in Lacey's direction. "Are you okay?"

"I'm afraid the bus going missing could have something to do with the fact that I was supposed to be on it." Lacey gestured toward herself. "I've had threats and stalkers in the past. It's very likely this whole thing is about me."

Cheryl fought to hold in a laugh, but it came out anyway. At least it wasn't loud. This girl was something else.

"Miss Landers," Riggins began. "I really don't think this has anything at all to do with you. I've already told you the woman who took your spot on that bus is dangerous."

"What exactly did she do?" Cheryl asked, unable to contain her curiosity.

The men exchanged a glance. "We're not really at liberty to say."

"I may need you to put a security detail on me," Lacey said. "What if the kidnappers realize I'm not there and come find me?" Her eyes widened with horror. "It's like some kind of movie."

Cheryl rolled her eyes. "I think you're fine. Go call your manager and see what he wants you to do."

Appeased for the moment, Lacey walked back to the car, her phone already pressed against her ear.

"What should we do to help?" Cheryl asked. "Do you want me to call our local police?" Chief Twitchell might not be too happy to hear from her, but the thought of scooping him on a case did give her some pleasure. The months since Cheryl had moved to Sugarcreek, she and the police chief hadn't always seen eye to eye on things, especially when Cheryl's curiosity got the better of her.

Riggins shook his head. "No. What we'd really like is to keep this quiet. Please don't mention the bus to anyone."

"But what if someone has seen it? Asking around could be very helpful in finding it. Sugarcreek is a small community…" Cheryl trailed off when she saw the stony expression on Riggins's face.

"For the safety of everyone on that bus, you need to keep it quiet. We'll handle it from here," he said gruffly.

"So that's it?" she asked. "We're just supposed to sit by and do nothing?"

"Not 'nothing.'" Naomi touched Cheryl's arm gently. "Now we pray about the outcome of the situation and for the safety of those involved."

Riggins nodded. "Thank you, ma'am." He turned to Cheryl and narrowed his eyes. "Not a word to anyone. We'll be in touch."

The two men started toward their vehicle.

"Wait!" Cheryl called, chasing after them. "I don't even know how to contact you. Do you have a card or something?"

Riggins frowned. "Let me look in the car." He scribbled a number on a scrap of paper from the console and handed it to her.

"Thank you," Cheryl said. "If I see or hear anything, I'll let you know." She waited for Detective Riggins to reciprocate her words, but he didn't.

"What a day," Levi said, coming up behind her. "It is hard to believe this happened."

Cheryl watched as Lacey danced around, holding her cell phone in the air for better service. "It sure is." She supposed the pop star was her responsibility for now.

"Are you okay?" Levi asked quietly.

"I feel like I'm to blame." Cheryl patted her hair. After frantically rushing around, she could only imagine how crazy it looked. "Those people got on that bus with complete trust that they'd arrive at their promised destination. And regardless of where they've ended up or why—they are definitely not where they're supposed to be."

"It's not your fault. I planned the weekend right along with you. There is no way we could have anticipated this happening."

Maybe Levi was right, but that didn't make Cheryl feel much better.

Seth and Naomi joined them next to Cheryl's car. "The bus could not have gone far," Seth commented. "Once they have all the authorities in the area looking, it will be found in no time."

"Do you think it is as the men said?" Naomi asked. "The bus is gone because of a woman onboard?" She nodded her head in Lacey's direction. The pop star still had the phone glued to her ear. "Or is it possible she may be right, and the whole thing is about her?"

Cheryl shrugged. "I guess anything is possible. But if it's about Lacey, surely they would've figured out by now that she isn't on the bus." She brightened. "Although I guess that would make things easier. Maybe they'll figure that out and ditch the bus and everyone on it somewhere safe."

Lacey sauntered over to the car. "Blake's freaking out." She rolled her eyes. "As usual."

"Would you like me to take you to the airport?" Cheryl asked. She didn't really want to make the drive to the nearest airport, but if it meant Lacey could go back to her own world, it might be worth it.

"Nope." Lacey shook her head. "Blake thinks I should lay low for a bit. I hope you don't mind a houseguest." She grinned. "I'm so sorry to impose like that, but I'd rather not check in to a hotel alone right now. I know those detectives say this whole bus thing has nothing to do with me, but until I'm sure, I can't risk it."

Cheryl stared. She had dirty dishes in the sink and the guest room wasn't exactly pop-star perfect right now. But she knew a losing battle when she saw one. "You aren't allergic to cats, are you?" She might not be thrilled with the prospect of a houseguest, but Beau would be.

"No. I'm more of a dog person," Lacey explained. "But cats are fine too."

"I guess it is all set then," Naomi said with a smile. "I think the two of you will get along just fine, and I have no doubt that bus will be found soon."

As Cheryl climbed in the car with Lacey, she hoped Naomi's words would prove true.

"So what is there to do here?" Lacey asked as they drove through Sugarcreek toward Cheryl's house. "It seems so...quiet."

Cheryl thought for a moment. "I can see how you might think that. I moved here a few months ago from Columbus, which is New York compared to Sugarcreek. At first it was a huge adjustment, and I wasn't completely sure I would stay." She slowed down as they neared a horse and buggy ahead of them in the road. "But I've come to realize life is what you make of it—wherever you may live.

I'm getting to know people around here, and the more friends I make, the busier I am."

"Like that cutie, Levi?" Lacey asked. "What's the deal there anyway?"

Cheryl's face grew hot. "There's not a deal. Levi is just a friend."

Lacey giggled. "I'll bet."

"So anyway," Cheryl said. "There are a lot of neat places to visit around the area. Flea markets, quaint little stores. Not to mention the food. The food is amazing."

"Nice change of subject," Lacey observed. "We'll discuss Levi more later."

That's what you think. Cheryl pulled the car into her driveway. "Here we are," she said. "Home sweet home."

"It's a cute little place. Kind of reminds me of my nana's house in Dover. That's where I used to visit growing up."

"Dover?" Cheryl asked. "That's only about twenty minutes from here. I had no idea you had ties to the area."

Lacey shrugged. "That's part of why I wanted to do the tour in the first place. Nana is in a retirement home not too far from here. I wanted to get in touch with my roots, so to speak, and also get a chance to see her and Papa." She sighed. "I haven't been able to visit much over these past few years."

Now things made a little more sense. All this time she'd thought how odd it was for Lacey to want to be in Sugarcreek. Why didn't Blake just tell her the whole truth about Lacey's desire to be on the tour? "I'm sure she'll be glad to see you." Once she'd shown Lacey around and introduced her to Beau, Cheryl settled at her laptop with a fresh cup of coffee. What a day this had been.

She had an e-mail from Aunt Mitzi, letting her know she'd be able to Skype early next week and wishing her well with the tour. She and her aunt tried to communicate at least once a week via Skype, but sometimes Aunt Mitzi wasn't able to get a signal. They e-mailed when they had the chance, although one of Cheryl's favorite things was when she had a real letter from her aunt. Even today, with technology literally at her fingertips all the time, there was something almost magical about receiving an honest-to-goodness snail-mail handwritten letter. And while Cheryl would love to sit down and pen a lengthy letter to her aunt, today she needed to get the information to her fast. So she'd settle for e-mail.

Aunt Mitzi,

I'm beginning to think this Live Like the Amish weekend was a mistake. We've had a pretty big setback, as the bus has gone missing. MISSING. How does that even happen? There are these FBI guys here who say it's because there's some old lady felon onboard, and I also have Lacey Landers staying at my house. You read that right. Lacey Landers! She and Beau are curled up right now watching a movie in the guest room. Thank goodness I put that old TV and DVD player in there or she'd be standing right beside me wanting to talk. I don't know that I've ever met anyone who talks as much as she does.

I am so concerned about the bus that I don't know how I'll be able to sleep. The detectives told me to stay out of it and let them handle it, and I could tell Levi and Seth felt the same way. Naomi and I have been involved with so many strange happenings over the past few months, I know they are probably right. But this time especially, I feel like I can't stand by and do nothing. Those detectives don't know anything about Sugarcreek. I don't know where they are from, but it's sure not around here.

I had a run-in with an old "friend" of yours named Richard Wellaby. He came to the store fit to be tied over the Live Like the Amish tour. Says it was his idea and we stole it. Kathy says you can commiserate with me and that you've dealt with him too. Yuck.

Oh—and Kathy has also enlisted my help in finding out some information about Heather's new beau. He's just passing through town, and she thinks there's something shady about him. I guess I'm getting a reputation for digging around and finding information... not sure if that's a good or bad thing!

Anyway, don't worry. I'll keep you posted. Hopefully by the time we get to Skype again, the bus will have been found and the biggest issue the group will have to face is too many fry-pie flavors, not enough time!

Love you!

Cheryl

She closed her laptop and took another sip of coffee. Maybe curling up in bed with a good book would take her mind off the missing bus and the missing people.

And the fact that she was the one who had brought them here and put them in danger in the first place. If anything happened to them... it would be all her fault.

Tomorrow Riggins and McGraw had better have some kind of lead. Otherwise, Cheryl was going to slip her detective hat back on and do some investigating of her own. She made a mental note to stop by the Honey Bee the next day. She needed to find out where Michael Rogers was staying anyway—and now she had another item on her agenda: find a busload of missing people.

Chapter Eight

The ringing phone brought Cheryl out of a deep sleep. "Hello," she mumbled.

"I know where it is," a deep voice said.

She sat up and pressed the phone closer to her ear. "Where what is?"

"Your busload of people."

Now she was fully awake. "Where is it? Who is this?"

"It's not missing for the reason you may think. I have to go now. But I'll be in touch."

"Wait! Please tell me where they are." Her words were too late. The caller had already hung up.

She checked her phone screen. The number was a local one, but she had no idea who it might be. She quickly searched the online White Pages for the number, but came up empty. Whoever it belonged to must be unlisted.

She got up and threw on her robe. Lacey was probably still snoozing, but Cheryl wanted to get to the store.

When Cheryl made her way into the living room, she was shocked to see that Lacey was already up and dressed and reading an old issue of *People* that had been in the recycle stack.

"Still an old lady, huh?" Cheryl asked, taking in her paisley dress and made-up face. The gray wig sat next to her on the couch.

Lacey grinned. "Yes, dearie," she said in a feeble voice. She picked up the wig and smoothed the gray curls. "Thankfully I had a little makeup in my purse. Most of my stuff was in the bag I left on the bus."

"I guess I should've thought to ask if you wanted to borrow some clothes or something. Some hostess I am."

"I think I'd rather stay in disguise," Lacey explained. "I'm still not convinced the bus disappearance didn't have anything to do with me, so I think I'd rather not be recognized."

"That makes sense." Cheryl reached down to rub Beau behind his ears. "But if you change your mind and want to borrow some clothes, let me know." Not that Cheryl's clothes would really fit Lacey. The woman was tiny. "Or if you want me to take you somewhere to buy some new clothes."

"I think I'll be okay. I may need to borrow your washing machine tonight though."

"Of course. Do you want anything for breakfast?"

"I helped myself to a Pop Tart already. Hope that's okay." Lacey held up a plate with just a few crumbs. "I'd forgotten how delicious those were."

"Yeah, I'm fresh out of smoothies and chia seeds."

Lacey gave a wry smile. "If you constantly had people reminding you not to gain an ounce, you'd do whatever you could to follow those instructions. My career kind of depends on it."

The only person who demanded Cheryl lose weight was Cheryl. And while that didn't always go as planned, at least her weight wasn't under public scrutiny. How difficult must that be? "Well I'll be glad to go and pick up some healthier options for you while you're here," Cheryl said. "I don't mind at all."

"That's okay." Lacey smiled mischievously. "I think it will be kind of nice to eat like a normal person for a couple of days. I can always work out extra hard when I get home."

"Suit yourself." Cheryl poured a cup of coffee in her to-go mug and returned to the living room. "I need to open the store. Esther will be there to work today, but there are a few things I need to get done. You're welcome to tag along if you'd like."

Lacey popped up from the couch. "Oh, that sounds like fun. Thanks."

"Beau goes with me a lot of days, but I think we'll be in and out of the Swiss Miss today, given the circumstances. I think he'd better stay here."

"He's a sweet cat. He makes me miss my dog. I have a dog sitter staying at my house while I'm gone, but I'm so used to him sleeping with me. I had a hard time sleeping last night."

"As did I. I couldn't stop thinking about all those people and where in the world they might be. I read until it was so late I couldn't help but close my eyes. As soon as I got into a deep sleep, my phone rang." She quickly filled Lacey in on the strange call she'd received.

"Wow," Lacey said. "That's crazy."

Cheryl ushered her out the door and closed and locked it behind them. "I know. I wish I knew what was going on."

"Did the voice sound familiar?" Lacey said as they climbed in the car.

"I think he was disguising it, so it's hard to say. Plus it was muffled, and he was talking pretty low. But if he's telling the truth, then maybe everyone is okay. That's the biggest worry for me. If they're all safe and sound, then that's all I care about."

"I know what you mean. I got to know some of them on the bus ride to Sugarcreek. They were really a fun group. There was this one couple on there, and they were so cute. Totally made me miss my nana and papa."

"In Dover." It still blew Cheryl's mind that Blake hadn't thought to tell her that Lacey had relatives in the area. He'd acted like it was all business.

"Yep. I haven't been able to go visit in over a year. It's been constant touring, filming, and photo shoots. Blake says we need to keep striking while the iron is hot. I've been in demand a lot since my last album went to number one." Her voice didn't convey as much happiness as Cheryl would've expected. "I grew up in Alabama. That's where my mom's family is from. Dad's side comes from this area. I spent way more time in Alabama than I did in Ohio—except that I'd spend three weeks with them every summer. Those were some great times."

"Do you get to go back to Alabama much?" Cheryl asked.

"It's been over a year for that too. I'm beginning to get homesick."

Cheryl couldn't imagine being away for that long. Even with her parents in Seattle, she still saw them as often as possible. And it seemed like with Lacey's income, money to fly back and forth wouldn't be an issue. "But aren't you in charge of your own schedule? Surely you can take a break whenever you want to."

"I have 'people' who do most of my booking." She used air quotes to emphasize the word. "And then on the rare days I actually have off, I'm so exhausted I can't bring myself to travel across the country. The only reason I wanted to come here was because I'm really nervous about this upcoming movie role. Since I grew up visiting my grandparents in Dover, I'd seen Amish people, but I never really knew any. I don't want to get to the movie set and totally get it wrong. I have a hard enough time being taken seriously as it is."

Perhaps Cheryl had misjudged her. She seemed like she genuinely wanted to do her best. "Must be a tough thing to always be away from your family. Are you planning to go visit them while you're here?"

Lacey nodded. "I'd planned to go on Saturday. Now I'm a little worried that my cover is blown. I suppose I'll just hire a driver to take me to Dover, and I'll stay disguised."

"I can give you a ride if you'd like. It's not far," Cheryl said. "I can drop you for the day or something."

"That would be wonderful. I haven't told them I'm here. I want it to be a surprise." She smiled. "And if all goes well, I'll have a week off before the movie begins shooting. I need to spend some time with the script, but I can certainly do that as well in Dover as I can anywhere else." She sighed. "I haven't told Nana about that either. I am afraid Blake will flip if I tell him I'm taking a week to spend with my family. I don't want her to get her hopes up."

"Do they come and visit you?"

Lacey shook her head. "They would love to, but Papa is in poor health and Nana doesn't want to leave him. It's so sweet. My aunts would totally take care of him, but Nana can't bear to leave his side."

"Sounds like a real love story."

"Yep. The everlasting kind. Rare these days."

And didn't Cheryl know it. After her breakup with Lance, she'd spent a lot of time trying to come to terms with staying single forever. She wasn't quite at peace about that yet. And she still hoped and prayed that true love would come her way. "Here we are," Cheryl said, pulling into a parking spot. "Esther will be in soon, and I'm betting Naomi will come with her. I can't wait to tell her about this morning's call."

"Are you going to call the detectives?" Lacey asked as they walked toward the Swiss Miss.

"Yes." She held up the slip of paper Riggins had scribbled on the day before.

They stepped inside the shop, and Cheryl inhaled. She still couldn't believe this was what she got to do every day. Each day brought new challenges and new faces through the door. It was such a refreshing change of pace from the banking career she'd left behind in Columbus.

"I'm kind of obsessed with these faceless Amish dolls," Lacey said, picking up one from a shelf. "I'm definitely going to take some back as gifts."

"Yeah, those are very popular. They're made locally by different women in the surrounding area."

"So neat."

The bell above the door jingled, and Esther and Naomi walked in. "Any word on the bus?" Naomi asked. "I could hardly sleep last night for wondering what had happened." She put a few jars of her homemade jam on the counter.

Cheryl filled them in on the phone call. "That's all that's happened. I tried to call Detective Riggins, but it was busy. I'll try him again in a few minutes. I wonder if they can somehow trace the call." She'd written the number on a piece of paper, and she set it down. "It seems kind of familiar, but I have no idea who it may belong to."

Esther peered at the number. "That number belongs to Lydia's family. They have a phone shanty at their house."

"Lydia's family?" Lydia Troyer was one of sixteen-year-old Esther's good friends. She worked part-time at the Swiss Miss and was also in rumspringa.

"Ja. Of course, Lydia uses her cell phone right now, so you may not have called her on the family line much."

The idea of rumspringa had taken Cheryl by surprise when she'd first arrived in Sugarcreek. It seemed so odd to watch Esther and Lydia wearing jeans and T-shirts and texting on cell phones just like other teenagers. "I do usually contact her on her cell, but I think I've actually called this number before. There's an answering machine, right?"

Esther nodded.

"I think we may drive out there and see if anyone asked any of the Troyers about using their phone." She turned to Esther.

"Do you think you can take care of things here for a little while?"

The girl nodded. "Ja. I expect it to be fairly quiet." January wasn't exactly prime tourist season, so she was probably right.

"What do you have planned?" Naomi asked. "Are you up to something?"

"You know me well," Cheryl said with a smile. "But I thought you might want to go too."

Naomi nodded. "Count me in."

"Well, I thought maybe we should go to the places the bus stopped yesterday to see if anyone working there remembers anything. Even one small detail could be the key to finding the bus." She smiled. "And we'll also stop by the Troyer home." She kept to herself the part about how she also planned to do a little more digging on Michael Rogers. Maybe Heather would be at the Honey Bee, and she would be forthcoming with information about her new flame.

"Sounds like a good plan." Naomi nodded.

Yesterday they'd only driven by the locations, and when the bus wasn't there, they'd moved on. Today, Cheryl wanted to inquire whether the bus had even stopped at the places it was supposed to. Since they hadn't kept the reservation at Dutch Valley, maybe they hadn't even stopped at any of the locations.

"Lacey, do you want to go with us?" Cheryl asked.

The girl nodded. "Sure." She frowned. "My phone is on its last leg. I may need to stop somewhere and buy a new charger if we don't find that bus and my bag soon."

Cheryl, Naomi, and Lacey got in the car. "The first place the bus was supposed to stop was By His Grace bookstore. Let's go see if the Berryhills can tell us anything."

Ray and Marion Berryhill were one of Cheryl's favorite couples. She always enjoyed being around them and hearing their tales of parenthood. They'd struggled for years to have a child and recently had been blessed with a baby girl.

"Hi, ladies," Ray greeted them. "Can I help you with something today?" Cheryl was a frequent visitor to the store, and he knew her favorite authors.

"Actually, I was hoping you might be able to tell me if the tour bus came by yesterday." She'd talked to Ray and Marion before the tour to be sure they'd be open and encourage them to offer some specials for the Live Like the Amish tour goers.

He nodded. "They sure did. They weren't here long though." He frowned. "But you know what's odd? You're the third group to come by and check on the bus."

"The third? Who else has checked?"

"Earlier today, two guys came in. They were both kinda gruff. One of them said something about his aunt being on the tour and he was trying to track her down." Ray frowned. "It seemed a little fishy to me. His eyes were shifty."

So Detectives McGraw and Riggins had concocted a story about an aunt? Why not just tell the truth? That they were detectives looking for a suspect. "I know those men. They were in the shop yesterday." She wasn't sure if she should fill Ray in on why the men were in Sugarcreek, so she remained silent. "Who else came by asking about the tour?"

Marion overheard and came over to the counter shaking her head. "That horrible Richard Wellaby. He came in yesterday afternoon just after the group left. He'd seen a sign out front that offered a discount for those on the tour."

"I'll bet that went over well."

Marion smiled. "Let's just say that Richard had some choice words to say about you. I believe he referred to you as 'Mitzi's niece, the idea-stealer' or something like that."

"Yeah, he came to the Swiss Miss yesterday morning and was pretty upset with me over the tour. He said it was his idea, and I had stolen it." Cheryl shook her head. "The funny thing is, I'd never even met him till yesterday. I certainly didn't know he'd planned a Live Like the Amish tour."

"Consider yourself lucky that you hadn't met him yet. We've all had a run-in with him at one time or another," said Ray. "What I don't understand is why someone who so clearly doesn't enjoy being around people would choose a life working with the public. First the store, then the tour company. Makes no sense."

"So many things don't," Cheryl said. She had one more question before they left. "How about the people in the tour group? Did you notice if any of them were acting odd yesterday?"

Ray and Marion exchanged a glance.

"Nothing *too* out of the ordinary," Ray said. "But one of the women seemed a little flustered. She had a phone with her that had a dead battery. She couldn't find the charger and asked if we sold them." He shrugged. "We don't, and when I told her that, she seemed very upset." He reached under the register and pulled out a purple cape. "In fact, she accidentally left this on the counter."

Cheryl recognized it as the one the woman the detectives were chasing had on yesterday. Had she left it on purpose?

"I see." Cheryl took the cape but found no identifying information in it.

"Why don't you take it? I know you'll be in touch with the tour group, and you can return it to the rightful owner." He grinned. "Besides, if it stays here much longer, Marion might take it home. She loves the color."

Cheryl and Naomi exchanged glances. She remembered Detective Riggins's plea that she not tell anyone about the missing bus. Should she heed his warning? Her conscience got the better of her, and she decided to keep the plight of the bus a secret.

"I'll take it and see that it gets returned." *If the bus itself ever returns.*

Lacey placed two books on the counter. Both were written by two of Cheryl's favorite authors. Lacey grinned at Cheryl's surprised expression. "Believe it or not, I do enjoy reading." She shrugged. "Besides, one of these is about an Amish woman and the other is set in Amish country. I figure I can mix business and pleasure."

Naomi and Cheryl waited while Lacey checked out then the three of them made their way back to the car. "I can't help but think the woman left that cape on purpose. She had it on when she came in to my store, along with a purple hat. She ditched the hat at my place. Then she ditched the cape at the next stop."

"But why?" Lacey asked.

"The purple cape and hat made her a target easy to spot. She must've known she was being followed or something, and by losing that stuff, she was able to blend in better."

"That makes sense," Naomi said. "And if she was looking to charge her phone, maybe she was calling someone for help."

"That is exactly what worries me," Cheryl said. "Maybe she had an accomplice in whatever crime she committed. And maybe they found her—and the tour bus."

"Try not to think the worst. Perhaps she was only trying to call her family or a friend. Remember that the detectives did not share with us what her supposed crime was. Maybe she is not so sinister as they would like us to believe."

True. Especially since Riggins had made up a story about his inquiry into the tour group. Why not tell Ray who he was and what he was doing? Cheryl started the car and headed toward the Honey Bee Café. "Hopefully the next stop will tell us more than that one. I mean, all we know at this point is that the old lady left her cape behind. That tells us that she probably knew she was being followed, but not much else."

"She must've had a gun or something," Lacey said.

"Why do you say that?"

She shrugged. "Why else would the bus driver have gone along with it? She was just a little old lady, right? So she must have done something pretty drastic to make him do what she said." Lacey smoothed her gray wig. "Unless it's like you say, and she called for help in the situation."

Lacey was right. Clearly the woman hadn't overpowered Mickey. He wasn't young, but he was a big, burly man. The scenarios that ran through her head about how he'd been forced to go against the scheduled route made her shudder.

She just hoped everyone was safe.

Chapter Nine

"A tour bus yesterday?" Heather asked. "Yeah, I remember them."

"Can you think of anything in particular that may have seemed odd?"

"Well the biggest thing that's odd is that you're the second person today to come in here and ask about them. What's up with that?"

Cheryl didn't even have to ask, but she did anyhow. "Who was here?"

"These two angry men. Seriously. They have anger management issues, I think. They were mean to me and hateful to each other. They had such bad attitudes, I pretty much didn't help them any."

"Well that's Riggins and McGraw to a T," Lacey piped up.

"Whoever they were, they were definitely upset." Heather sighed. "But anyway, the only thing I know about that tour group was that I had to make twenty-four coffees. It took a while, and the bus driver kind of got annoyed. But then..." She trailed off.

"Then what?"

"It was weird. He got a phone call on his cell phone, and it seemed like an argument."

Cheryl didn't know Mickey that well, but each time she'd been around him, he'd seemed pretty easygoing. "Any idea what it was about?"

"I have no clue. The only thing I really heard him say was that he didn't like it and wasn't sure about something." She shrugged. "I know that's like, totally unhelpful, but that's all I remember."

"No, that's good information," Cheryl said. "I appreciate your help."

"What's all the fuss about anyway? Was there someone famous on that bus or something?"

Lacey coughed.

"I organized the tour and just wanted to follow up on it," Cheryl said. It was the closest thing to an explanation she could offer at this point. "Thank you so much, and if you think of anything else, please let me know." Cheryl looked around. She didn't see Michael. Had he left town already? "How was your date last night?"

Heather blushed. "We had a very nice time. I showed him around Sugarcreek. He loved all the farmland around here and said he'd always wanted a farm of his own."

Michael hadn't seemed like the kind of guy who'd belong on a farm, but Cheryl hated to judge. "That's nice. Is he sticking around awhile?"

"A couple of weeks, I think." Heather looked at her suspiciously. "Why?"

"He mentioned he may want to stop by the store for a few souvenirs. Be sure and tell him to get some of Naomi's jam."

"Will do," said Heather.

Once they were in the car, Lacey burst out laughing. "I so wanted to tell her who I was when she wondered if there was someone famous on the bus. Sadly though, the only thing famous on that bus is my bag."

Cheryl groaned.

"Seriously. It's one of a kind." Lacey grinned.

"Well that wasn't all that helpful either, except I'm relieved to learn that Riggins and McGraw have at least been retracing the bus's stops." Cheryl pulled out her phone and called Riggins again.

"Broadway Pizza, can I help you?"

"I must have a wrong number." She hung up and looked at Riggins's scrawled handwriting again then redialed.

"Broadway Pizza," the perky voice said again.

Cheryl hit the End button and leaned her head against the seat. "I'm beginning to think he didn't want me to be able to reach him."

"Maybe it was just a mistake. Surely you will hear from him soon," Naomi said.

Cheryl headed toward the Troyers' place. "Do you know Lydia's parents?" she asked.

"Ja. I have known them since before Esther and Lydia were even born."

"There's the phone shanty," Cheryl said as she pulled into the driveway.

Lacey giggled. "It kinda looks like an outhouse."

"I thought the same thing when I moved here," Cheryl explained. "But actually it's kind of a phone booth. It's a way for the family to get in touch with people if they need to or if there's an emergency. It's also for the family business. There's even an answering machine."

"Cool. I think I remember my nana having one of those."

Cheryl wasn't too much older than Lacey, but at that moment she felt ancient. "There's Thomas. I'll ask him if anyone asked to use their phone this morning."

Thomas waved as she approached. "Hello, Cheryl."

She smiled. "I have an odd question for you. Someone called me this morning from your phone shanty. Do you know if anyone asked to use it? It was pretty early."

He rubbed his chin. "Not that I know of. Daed may know, but he is not here right now."

"Do you keep it locked?" she asked.

Thomas widened his eyes. "No. I guess we have never had a problem before with someone using the phone. Did whoever called you scare you or something?"

"No. But they also didn't tell me their name. I just wondered if you may know." She told him good-bye and climbed back in the car. "Well that's a bust." She sighed and started the engine. "They don't lock it, so anyone could've made that call."

"I was afraid of that," Naomi said. "They live so far out here, I could not imagine them locking it."

"Right. But that makes me think whoever made that call is familiar with the area. How else would they know about the Troyers' phone?" She sighed. "How about we go to lunch?"

"I'm totally starving."

Cheryl glanced at Naomi. "Do you need to get home now?"

Naomi shook her head. "Now that I don't have a bus full of people at my house, I guess I don't have anything to rush back for." She smiled. "Except for chores, and those will be there when I get home."

Cheryl laughed. "I guess they will."

"So did you want all those people at your farm?" Lacey asked once they were seated at Beachy's Restaurant. "The description of our activities sounded really great."

Naomi sighed. "I was the last one to give my support to the tour," she explained. "Seth, Levi, and the girls thought it would be fun, and Cheryl was all for it, but I was worried the group would be bored or would feel like we were putting them to work too much."

"Oh, I think it sounded lovely," Lacey said.

"I even told Mickey that I thought we should have an escape plan in case they all hated it. I had already arranged with him to take the group to the flea market if things weren't going well."

"You should've told me you were so worried about it," Cheryl said. "I didn't realize it was causing you trouble."

"I would not say 'trouble.' I just wanted to be sure they were all happy with the tasks we'd chosen for them, and so I made sure there was a plan in place for those who were unhappy."

The waitress stopped by their table to take their order. Cheryl and Naomi ordered the lunch special, meatloaf with green beans.

The waitress turned to Lacey. "And for you?" she asked.

"I'll take the chicken pot pie, mashed potatoes, and gravy," Lacey said in a British accent. "And go ahead and put me down for a slice of pecan pie."

Cheryl shook her head at the girl's accent. What was she doing?

The waitress walked away, and Lacey giggled. "Do you think she really thought I was an old British lady?"

Naomi laughed along with her. "You were very convincing."

"That's my job." She leaned forward as if to tell them a secret. "Sometimes I do that when I go to a new place and no one knows me. I take all these voice classes to help me with different accents and stuff. It's always fun to try them out on real people."

Cheryl fought to keep from rolling her eyes as Lacey continued to use her accent the rest of the meal.

"Tell me your favorite thing about living in Sugarcreek," she said to Naomi.

Naomi thought for a moment. "That's an easy one for me. My family is here. My home. My church." She smiled. "I'd never want to be anywhere they are not."

"Cool." Lacey bit into a roll. "This is so good. I don't remember the last time I had carbs. I think I've been missing out on the good parts of life."

"What is your life like in California?" Naomi asked.

Lacey stopped eating for a moment. "Honestly? It's the opposite of what you just described about your life in Sugarcreek. My closest friends are people I grew up with—not people I met in Hollywood. I have a dog who is my constant companion. And my manager. A trainer. An assistant. A dog sitter. A housekeeper." She sighed. "But I think being surrounded by friends and family would be lovely."

"Sorry about that," Cheryl said to Naomi when Lacey left the table to go wash her hands. "I didn't know we'd be having lunch with an elderly British lady."

"I think she is a funny girl," Naomi said. "Such a zest for life. No need to apologize." She raised her eyebrows at Cheryl. "She seems rather lonely to me—so young to tackle so many things without a family surrounding her. How is it going, having her stay with you?"

Cheryl shrugged. "It's fine. She really wasn't any trouble, and Beau seems to love her. Believe it or not, she even has ties to the area. Her grandparents are in a retirement home near Dover. She grew up visiting them during the summers. I guess that's part of the reason she wanted to come on the tour in the first place—to come back to her roots a little."

"That is nice. I think you should give her a chance," Naomi urged. "She could turn out to be a good friend."

Doubtful, but stranger things had happened. Like a bus vanishing into thin air.

Lacey made her way back to the table. "This place is so cute," she exclaimed. "I can't tell you the last time I was able to eat a meal without photographers waiting outside." She leaned against the booth.

"Hopefully you will not have to deal with that here," Naomi said kindly. "We have had a few celebrities here in Sugarcreek for visits and for filming in the area, and I think they all had good experiences."

"I hope you're right," Lacey said. "The movie I'll be doing next will actually be filming near here. So it will be nice to get the lay of the land before the shoot begins."

The waitress stopped at their table then and put heaping platters of food in front of them, putting an end to their conversation. Once they were done eating, they made a quick stop at the Dollar General so Lacey could get a new phone charger.

"Look at the horse and buggies parked right there with the cars," she exclaimed. "That's so cool."

Most of the restaurants and stores in Sugarcreek had parking spots for vehicles as well as posts for horse and buggy parking. Cheryl had been there long enough that it seemed normal to her, but she could understand that it must be a bit of culture shock for Lacey.

Lacey returned to the car, a gleeful expression on her face. "I'll be so glad to plug this in," she said. "I'm sure Blake is freaking out since my phone died this morning."

"He keeps pretty close tabs on you, doesn't he?" Cheryl asked. Just one more reason she wouldn't have been cut out for a life in Hollywood. She was far too independent to tolerate someone keeping track of her every move.

Lacey nodded. "He does. As he says—I'm his meal ticket." She laughed. "It's not as horrible as it sounds. But he gets a cut of everything I make, so I guess it's in his best interest to keep close tabs on me."

Either way, it sounded miserable to Cheryl. "Naomi, do you want us to take you home? Or back to the Swiss Miss?"

"To the store will be fine. I'm hopeful you'll hear from your detective friends soon."

Cheryl laughed. "I'm pretty sure 'friends' is an overstatement. I am beginning to doubt that Riggins will call me even if he finds the bus. Never mind that I was the one who advertised the tour in the first place."

They made their way to the Swiss Miss and greeted Esther.

"Has anyone been by looking for me?" Cheryl asked.

Esther shook her head. "No. It has been a very slow day. A woman came in for some of Maam's preserves though and bought three jars."

"It's my best seller," Cheryl bragged as Naomi's cheeks turned pink. "One lady came in a couple of weeks ago and practically bought out the whole stock. She said her husband adores the stuff."

Naomi smiled. "I am glad your customers enjoy it."

Lacey let out a loud gasp from the corner. She had her phone plugged in, and from the way she was holding it to her ear, she'd clearly gained enough battery to check her messages. "They know I'm here."

"What?" Cheryl asked. "Who knows?"

Lacey sighed and sank on to the floor. "Blake sent me a text an hour ago that says my being in Sugarcreek has shown up on a couple of social media sites. If it's confirmed that I'm here, the paparazzi will be all over the place."

Naomi walked over and knelt down in front of her. "It will be okay." She placed a hand on Lacey's shoulder. "So far it sounds as if it is just rumors about your being here. As long as you stay in disguise, I think you will be fine."

Lacey's face grew pale as she flipped through her messages. "Some guy sent me an e-mail directly. He asked if I was enjoying the fresh country air and time away from the city."

"What guy?" Cheryl asked.

"There's a guy who has tried to contact me a few times, but he's always gone through Blake. Says he just wants to talk. He's never made any real threats, but somehow he managed to get one of my personal e-mail addresses. 'Fresh country air?' 'Time away from the city?'" She looked up from the screen. "It sounds like he knows where I am."

Cheryl had to admit—it did seem odd. But she didn't want to alarm Lacey. She might come across as feisty and independent, but Cheryl picked up on her fear. Being a public figure must feel so vulnerable sometimes. "Or maybe he just saw the reports on social media and is trying to get you to tip him off? Fresh country air describes Sugarcreek but also about a million other places. So until this guy says something threatening or tells you he saw you here, I don't think you should worry too much. Maybe just forward it to Blake and have him handle it?" Although she wasn't sure how capable Blake was.

Lacey gave a feeble smile. "I hope you're right. But how did he get my address in the first place? Just in case people have figured out I'm here, maybe I should just try a new disguise." She stood up and dusted off her dress. "I need to blend in more."

"There's a thrift store across the street," Cheryl suggested. "Would you like to go over there and pick up something else to wear?"

"I think that's a great idea!" Lacey seemed energized again. "I'll be back in a jiffy." She grabbed her phone and her wallet and walked out the door.

"The last thing we need is for there to be a bunch of media here sniffing around," Cheryl said. "That's a surefire way for news of the bus disappearance to get out. At first I was really irritated that Riggins wanted us to keep that quiet, but I wonder if maybe that is best. Maybe the best way to keep the people safe is for the culprit to think no one is looking for them."

"That makes sense." Naomi nodded. "What about Lacey? Do you think she is in danger?"

Cheryl shrugged. "I don't know. I don't like that there are reports out there claiming she's in Amish country. Or that some guy who has tried to contact her in the past somehow got his hands on her e-mail address and is making vague claims like he knows her whereabouts. But I still think she's safe here. Her disguise was actually pretty good. Someone would have to know she was here masquerading as an old lady to be tipped off. So unless they already have that knowledge, even if they're here looking for her, I think she's going to stay hidden. Today at lunch, I definitely don't think the waitress thought she was waiting on Lacey Landers. I think she thought she was waiting on an old lady."

"An old, British lady." Naomi chuckled.

"Of course. How could I forget?" Cheryl busied herself around the store, straightening shelves and double-checking a couple of orders that should be in soon. "I hate not knowing what's going on," she said finally. "I'm starting to think Detective Riggins gave me that pizza parlor number on purpose."

"Not being able to get in contact with him certainly is frustrating," Naomi admitted. "But perhaps we can come up with a plan of our own in the meantime."

Before Cheryl could answer, the door opened and a young Amish girl stepped inside.

"Can I help you?" Cheryl asked.

"I can't believe it," Lacey asked excitedly. "You bought it. Do I look authentic or what?"

Cheryl widened her eyes in horror, but Naomi burst out laughing.

"From a distance you could pass as a local, but up close there is still a little work to do. If it were not for the hair and the makeup, you'd have me fooled." Naomi smiled.

"Except for that iPhone." Cheryl shook her head. She glanced at Naomi. Her friend didn't look offended but amused. Maybe it would be okay after all. She didn't know why she felt so responsible for Lacey, but she did.

"I guess I should probably put that in my purse, huh?" Lacey asked sheepishly.

"Might not be a bad idea," Cheryl said with a smile. She straightened the shelf by the entrance door. "Naomi and I were just discussing the bus situation."

"Any ideas?"

"I have several questions," Naomi began. "Mainly centering around this mysterious woman in purple. Where did she come from? Did she even mean to join the tour?"

Cheryl shook her head. "I don't believe so. She ran in here so flustered." She thought for a minute. Flustered might not even be the right description. "Actually, thinking back, she seemed frightened." She shook her head. "I never in a million years would've suspected her of being a criminal. And I also wonder who she was trying to call from the bookstore. If we only knew for sure if she'd gotten in touch with anyone, we'd know if she acted alone."

"That is just it. I am still not convinced the woman had anything to do with it. What do we really know for sure?" Naomi asked.

"We know the bus made two stops. We know there was nothing unusual about their bookstore visit, except for the woman shedding her cape. The visit to the Honey Bee Café seems like it went pretty smoothly as well, except for Mickey's odd phone call."

"And then...poof, they vanished," Lacey finished.

"So where exactly do we go next?" Cheryl asked. "I'm kind of at a loss."

"How about whatever lies between the coffee shop and the Millers' farm?" Lacey asked. "Maybe even if they didn't stop, someone saw them drive past. If we can figure out which direction they went once they left the coffee shop, then maybe we can follow that road until we find something concrete."

Cheryl frowned. She should've thought of that plan. After all, she'd been the one sharpening her detective skills ever since she moved to Sugarcreek.

"That sounds like a goot plan," Naomi said.

Lacey grinned. "Let me wash this old-lady makeup off my face and put my hair in a proper bun, and we'll go see what we can find out."

Chapter Ten

"Let's drive on past the Honey Bee Café just as the bus would've done when it left there. We'll see what we come to next," Cheryl said once they were loaded in her car. Thank goodness for sweet Esther, who didn't mind tending the store alone. And thank goodness for a slow January day that gave Cheryl the time to search for a missing bus.

"It looks like the Glick place is the first farm we pass along this route," Naomi observed. "It is up here on the right."

Cheryl slowed the car and pulled into the driveway at the Glicks'. A picturesque farmhouse sat at the end of the driveway with the remnants of a large garden next to it.

"Look at that laundry hanging on the line," Lacey exclaimed as they exited the car. "I can't imagine doing it that way, especially in January, but it's so cute. I'll bet it smells really fresh too."

Cheryl silenced her with a glance. "Remember, you're trying to pass yourself off as an Amish girl. Don't act like everything you see is a novelty or Mrs. Glick will think something is off."

"Ja," Lacey said. "But you are right." Her imitation of Naomi's slight accent was spot-on.

Cheryl cringed until she heard Naomi stifle a laugh.

Martha Glick greeted them at the door and welcomed them inside, something Cheryl was confident had to do with Naomi's presence. "Thanks for inviting us in," Cheryl said once they were seated in the living room. "Your home is lovely." Even after months in Amish country, she still enjoyed being welcomed into their homes. The Glicks' living room had gleaming hardwood floors and a fireplace that offered a welcome respite from the chilly outdoor temperatures.

"Would you like something to drink?" Martha asked.

"No thank you," Naomi said. "We can't stay long." She smiled warmly. "But whatever you're cooking smells wonderful."

"Danki. I am trying to get a head start on dinner." Martha smoothed the apron she wore over her plain dark purple dress. "What can I help you with?"

"You may have heard about the Live Like the Amish weekend that is taking place," Cheryl began.

Martha nodded. "I have heard about it. It is this weekend, is it not? How is it going?"

Cheryl and Naomi exchanged a glance. They'd already decided that honesty was the best policy with Martha. Naomi knew her well enough to know that she could be trusted not to tell everyone in town that the bus was missing.

Cheryl took a deep breath. "The bus has gone off its scheduled course. It was supposed to be at the Millers' farm yesterday afternoon, and it never showed up." Saying the words out loud made the whole situation feel more hopeless than it already had.

Martha's eyes widened. "That does not sound good."

"They were at the Swiss Miss on schedule and made a couple of other stops. But since then, we haven't seen a trace." Cheryl shook her head. "And to further complicate it, there has been no contact from anyone on the bus. Most of them had cell phones, including the driver. But we haven't heard from any of them." From the corner of her eye, she could see Lacey start to fidget, probably thinking of her long-lost bag on the bus.

"That is worrisome. Do you have any ideas where they may be?" Martha asked.

"We were hoping maybe you'd seen the bus go past here," Cheryl explained. "It would've been yesterday afternoon."

"You are the second group who has been here asking if I saw a bus go past yesterday," Martha said. "Two men were here this morning with the same question, although they didn't tell me it was your tour bus. They said they were detectives."

So Riggins and McGraw had changed tactics since yesterday. Were they more desperate or had they thought Martha would be more forthcoming if she knew their official capacity? The news they'd thought to stop at the Glicks' place should've brought Cheryl peace that at least they were following every lead, but instead she felt strangely jealous they'd thought of it first.

"They're trying to keep the disappearance under wraps," Cheryl said. "It's for the safety of everyone on board."

"Well, I'll tell you the same thing I told them—I was baking and doing laundry, and I wasn't outside to see any bus go past." She paused. "But there was one thing I didn't tell them."

Cheryl leaned forward. "What's that?"

"My two boys were out playing in the yard after school." Martha smiled. "You see, those two men were so rude and seemed untrustworthy to me. I answered their question honestly—I wasn't in the yard. But I didn't want to get Ike and Chester involved." She stood. "Besides, they were at school this morning anyway. They're in the backyard now though, and I'll get them."

Once Martha was gone, Lacey came to life. "This place is so cool," she exclaimed. "It smells so yummy, and I am totally pumped to be here. This will really help me feel authentic in my movie."

"Do you always like to do research before you portray a character in a movie?" Naomi asked.

Lacey giggled. "Well the last movie I was in, I played a girl trying to make it as a pop star. It didn't require much research." She grew somber. "This role was a long shot for me. It's a romantic comedy, but on the serious side. I really want to prove to all the haters that I am a real actress."

"I think it sounds like you are well on your way." Naomi gave a reassuring smile.

Martha ushered Ike and Chester into the room. The twin boys looked to be about five, and Cheryl thought for the millionth time since moving to Sugarcreek that Amish children were some of the cutest she'd ever seen in the world.

"Boys, Miss Cooper wants to ask you about something that happened yesterday afternoon. Think carefully before you answer."

"Yes, ma'am," they said in unison.

Cheryl was almost certain the whole room could hear her biological clock ticking. At thirty and with no husband on the horizon, she tried hard to push thoughts of a family of her own from her head. She trusted that God had a plan for her life, but whether it included marriage and children, she did not know. She knelt down so she was on Ike's and Chester's level. "Yesterday after school, were you playing outside in the yard?"

Ike nodded. "We were playing ball. Chester is better at kicking it, but I'm faster." He grinned, showing off a gap in his front teeth.

"That sounds like so much fun." She smiled. "While you were playing, did you see a bus drive past your house?"

The boys looked at each other then nodded. "We saw it," said Chester. "It was silver like a nickel."

"Do you remember when it drove past?" Did five-year-olds have any concept of time? Cheryl worried the question was too hard. "Was it right after you got home from school, or had you been playing for a while?"

"We had just started playing ball. And we started playing as soon as we got home from school." Chester looked pleased with himself at having answered her question.

"Very good." Cheryl smiled encouragingly. "One more question. Do you remember which way it was going?"

"Thata way." Ike pointed in the direction of the Millers' farm.

Cheryl, Naomi, and Lacey thanked the Glicks for their help and made their way to the car. "So somewhere between here and your house, the bus went off track." Cheryl sighed. It was like putting together a puzzle that had several missing pieces.

"That does not help us much, does it?" Naomi asked.

"Why?" Lacey piped up from the backseat. "We know we're headed the right way."

"There is a main thoroughfare between here and there. Which means they probably took it because we certainly did not see them go past our house," Naomi explained. "And from that road, there is no end to where they could have gone."

"So we're kind of back to square one?" Lacey asked, the disappointment evident in her voice.

"Not totally. At least we have a direction. And a time frame." Cheryl turned out of the driveway and headed toward the Swiss Miss. "That's more than we had when we started."

"Do you think the people on the bus are scared?" Lacey asked quietly. "I hate to think of them being scared. But I know I would be."

Cheryl had been thinking the same thing. "They spent the night somewhere last night. I wonder where?"

"Most of them brought some kind of blanket with them," Lacey said. "I know that was one of the things that was listed as optional to pack, but I know a lot of them had blankets and pillows because they took naps on the way from the airport. So at least no matter where they were, they had some of the comforts of home. I travel a lot for work, and I almost always take my own blanket and pillow. That way no matter where I am in the world, I feel a little more at home. So I'm sure they're fine."

"The whole thing just makes me so mad. And those two detectives… I've half a mind to go straight to the police chief and tell him what's going on."

"What's stopping you?" Naomi asked. "Are you secretly hoping you will get to the bottom of things without bringing Chief Twitchell in?"

Perhaps the thought had crossed Cheryl's mind. But only briefly. "I wish I knew if Riggins was right, that if we let everyone around here know about the disappearance, it will harm the situation rather than help it. I'm very torn."

"For what it's worth, I think you should try calling him again," Lacey said. "If you still don't get him, then let's call it what it is—a fake number." She giggled. "I've given out enough fake numbers, but I'm no detective. You'd think they'd be on the up-and-up."

"Sounds good." Cheryl pulled into a space near the Swiss Miss. "If I don't reach him this time, then it's time to really consider going to the local authorities. Surely there is some kind of jurisdiction. It seems like the federal agents would need to work with the local authorities in some capacity anyway."

"There's also always the chance that Riggins and McGraw have already done that and just chose to keep you out of the loop," Lacey pointed out. "They didn't seem too interested in your input yesterday. Maybe they've already alerted your local chief."

"Maybe." Cheryl unbuckled her seat belt. "But it seems like if they had, someone would've contacted me for more information by now. A list of the passengers, their next of kin, something."

"And you have that information?" Naomi asked.

Cheryl nodded. "I sure do. It's saved in a file on my laptop."

They got out of the car and went inside the Swiss Miss. Esther had the place to herself. "We've had a few customers," she said. "And Ben and Rueben played checkers for a little while."

Cheryl grinned. "Of course." The two brothers showed up to the Swiss Miss nearly every day to engage in a rousing game of checkers. At first she'd been stunned that they didn't speak to one another, but she'd since learned more about them and now found their regular games endearing. They'd recently taken steps toward reconciliation, but their time together was still pretty quiet. Ben left the Amish faith years ago, and by meeting at the store and playing checkers, it gave the brothers a chance to still have some kind of relationship.

"Thanks so much for your help, Esther. You're a good employee."

Esther beamed. "Danki."

Cheryl pulled out her cell phone and dialed Riggins's number again.

"Thanks for calling Broadway Pizza. How can I help you?"

"Sorry. Wrong number." She set the phone down on the counter and sighed. "Well, ladies. It seems like we have a decision to make. Trust Riggins or contact the local authorities?"

As she was finishing the sentence, the Swiss Miss door burst open. A handsome man with dark hair hurried toward the counter. "No authorities, please." He stopped when he reached Cheryl. "At least not until I know what's going on. My grandmother's life may depend on it."

Chapter Eleven

"I'm Roy Neal." He reached into his coat pocket and pulled out a badge. "I'm with the FBI, and I'm looking for a missing person." His dark hair was a perfect contrast with his blue eyes. He had just enough stubble on his face to be considered rugged and a tiny scar above his right eyebrow.

"I think I've heard this one too many times recently." Cheryl tried to get a read on him to see if he was shady, but his gaze was unwavering.

"What do you mean?"

"Yesterday two men came in, Detectives Riggins and McGraw. They made the same claim. How do I know you are who you say you are?" Her gut told her she could trust him, but it had also once told her to trust that she'd spend the rest of her life with Lance. So maybe it was faulty sometimes.

"I'll do whatever I need to do in order for you to verify my credentials." He handed her his badge and pulled a business card from his wallet. "Here is a phone number you can call and check out. It's to the field office I work out of, and they'll be able to validate what I'm saying."

Cheryl peered closely at the badge. It did look authentic. She read the card. "Okay, Mr. Neal. I'll play along. Hold on just a minute while I make the call." She wasn't sure what to think. Three detectives in small Sugarcreek? It didn't seem right.

After talking a few minutes with Mr. Mangun in the field office, she returned to the counter. "Your story checks out." She handed Roy his badge. "But why aren't you working with the other two agents who are investigating?"

Roy narrowed his eyes. "Other two agents?"

Cheryl nodded. "Detectives Riggins and McGraw. Sorry I don't know their first names. They haven't exactly been super friendly. In fact, today they're MIA." She pulled the slip with Riggins's number on it from her pocket and slapped it on the counter. "The number they gave me to contact them is for some pizza joint."

Roy frowned. "It may be worse than I thought."

"Worse? What do you mean?"

"As far as I know, there are no detectives named Riggins and McGraw. I believe those may be the men who are after my grandmother."

"Hold on." Lacey held up her hand to stop him. "I am totally confused. Can you, like, start at the beginning? Who is your grandma?"

Despite the tense situation, Cheryl stifled a laugh at Roy's expression. She had to admit, the contrast between Lacey's Amish-girl look and her Valley-girl speech was a little amusing.

"Yes, please," Cheryl said to Roy. "Can you fill us in on what you're doing here?"

He nodded. "I've been in Canada for the past week. I had some time off and just needed to get away." He took a breath. "I got this weird call from my grandma yesterday morning. She was driving and said that there were two men following her."

"Riggins and McGraw?" Cheryl asked.

Roy shrugged. "I guess. If that's even their names."

Lacey tapped his arm. "Go on."

"Anyway, at first I just thought she was being paranoid. But then while I was on the line with her, they broadsided her. Thankfully she kept her wits and was able to keep control of the car."

"That is terrible," Naomi said. "She must have been so scared."

He nodded. "She was terrified. Once I realized someone was really after her, I tried to help her figure out what to do. She was nearly to the Sugarcreek exit. I told her to take the exit and go to the police station. She hung up so she could concentrate, and I expected to hear from her shortly. The call never came."

"What time was that?" Cheryl asked.

"Just before lunch yesterday. When I never heard from her again, I called your local police station. They hadn't seen her but promised to be on the lookout." He frowned. "Did you see her here?"

"She came running in just before lunchtime yesterday. She seemed a little flustered when she got here, but she calmed down once we started talking." Cheryl recalled the brief conversation she'd had with the woman. "She ended up joining a tour group that was in the store at the time—a Live Like the Amish tour that's going on at a local farm until Monday."

Roy sighed with relief. "So you saw her, and she's okay? And now she's with a group at an Amish farm?" He grinned. "That's the most welcome news I've heard in a long time."

Cheryl and Naomi exchanged a glance. "I'm afraid there's more to the story than that," Cheryl began. "The bus your grandma got on never made it to its destination. We don't know where it is now."

Roy sank on to a nearby stool. "You mean the whole bus disappeared? With my grandma onboard?"

Lacey went to his side in a flash. "Yes, but don't worry. We've been retracing the stops. We're searching for it." She patted his back. "Would you like some water or something? You look a little pale."

Cheryl was rendered speechless, watching the girl in action. Bring in a handsome guy in distress, and Lacey turned into some kind of compassionate Florence Nightingale.

Roy managed a smile. "That would be great, thanks."

The megawatt smile he got in return practically burned Cheryl's retinas. "You're welcome. I'm Lacey, by the way. Lacey Landers." She lowered her voice. "I'm not really Amish, but I have been in disguise because I thought I might be in danger, considering the bus disappearance and all." Lacey filled him in on the events of the previous day and her involvement. "And you know what? Since the bus disappearance clearly had something to do with your grandma, I can go back to my regular clothes now!"

Naomi shook her head. "I do not believe it is that simple."

"Right," Cheryl agreed. "If Roy's grandma isn't a criminal, then she is a victim. Riggins and McGraw are after her for some reason. So she couldn't have been the reason the bus disappeared because Riggins and McGraw don't know where it is either."

Lacey wrinkled her nose. "So the bus disappearing could have something to do with me after all?" she asked quietly.

Cheryl shrugged. "I guess at this point there is no real way to know. So for the time being, it may be best for you to stay in disguise."

Lacey looked disappointed, but agreed.

"Why were the men after your grandma?" Cheryl asked.

"I have no idea and neither did she. She said she'd never seen them or their car before. She'd been at the park yesterday, taking a walk before her book club meeting. When she got in her car and pulled out of the parking lot, they pulled out behind her. She realized they were following her and didn't go home. Instead she got on the interstate and called me."

"So odd." Cheryl chewed on her lip for a moment. "We're back to square one on the bus disappearance though. Because McGraw and Riggins had us convinced they were FBI and your grandma was the reason the bus disappeared, we didn't really consider any other possibilities."

"Did you contact the local authorities?" Roy asked.

"The detec— I mean, the two men asked us not to. They said they'd handle the investigation. But I guess what they were really doing was trying to find your grandma. For some reason."

"And there's no way my grandma had anything to do with a whole bus disappearing. She's just a sweet little old lady. She used to be a librarian, and now she is retired. My grandpa passed away a few years back, and my parents live in Florida now. We wanted her to move to a retirement home, but Grandma refused to leave her house. She said she'd lived there her whole adult life, and she'd just stay put." He raked a hand through thick brown hair. "I'm relieved those guys didn't catch up with her, but not knowing where she is now is worrying me."

Lacey nodded, a solemn expression on her face. "I can't imagine how you feel." She leaned toward him conspiratorially. "I'm very close to my nana too. I'd be so worried if she were in this situation."

"Should I call our local police chief?" Cheryl asked.

Roy stood. "I'll go by there in just a bit and explain the situation. I've already spoken to him on the phone, but he didn't seem too concerned since he had no proof Grandma was even here." He motioned toward the door. "I saw her vehicle parked out front though, which is what led me to your store. I'm about to go see if it's unlocked and if so, if there's anything unusual inside."

"Can I help?" Cheryl asked. She was intrigued by the innocent-looking woman who had done something to cause two goons to chase her.

"Sure." Roy smiled then turned to Lacey. "Everyone can come help."

Clearly even dressed in plain clothing, Lacey managed to capture hearts.

They followed Roy outside and to an older model maroon Buick. "See that?" Roy asked, pointing at the driver's side door. "Looks like someone jimmied the lock to get in."

"And there are scrapes and a dent on the passenger side where they must've sideswiped her." Cheryl peered inside the car. "It does look like someone went through the glove box and the console. There are papers and Kleenex scattered all over."

"I'm guessing this is the work of your 'detectives.'" Roy made air quotes with his fingers as he said the word. "I can't imagine what they were looking for though. What could my grandma possibly have gotten into that's causing such a fuss?"

"I don't know, but the only way we are ever going to know is if we find her before they do," Cheryl said.

"Tell you what," Roy began, "how about you drive me along the route they were supposed to be on? I'd like to see it for myself."

"Esther and I will stay at the store," Naomi said to Cheryl. "I'll help her tidy up so you can close when you get back." She said her good-byes and hurried back inside.

Cheryl, Lacey, and Roy piled into Cheryl's car. She explained the route the bus had taken and what they'd learned at the Glicks' farm. "The bus definitely went past there, but it didn't make it all the way to the Millers'."

"What I don't understand is why none of the tour attendees have called to let their families know what happened. I've been calling Grandma repeatedly, but it just goes to voice mail."

"I'll bet I can answer that," Lacey piped up. "When we got off the bus at the Swiss Miss, the bus driver asked everyone to put their phones in a box. He said it was to preserve the authenticity of the weekend. Everyone called or texted their families, letting them know they made it to Sugarcreek, then put their phones in the box as we stepped off the bus. We weren't supposed to get them back until Monday afternoon on the bus ride back to the airport."

Cheryl slowed the car to turn on to the main road. "But you have your phone with you. Did you refuse to participate?"

Lacey giggled. "Well, I have two phones. I put my backup phone in the box and kept my main phone with me. I wanted an authentic weekend and all, but I still wanted to communicate with the outside world."

"I see," Cheryl said. She glanced at Roy. "We learned earlier that your grandmother's cell phone was dead. She was looking for a charger when she went to the bookstore. She tried to buy one there, but they didn't have one. So it's possible that she couldn't have contacted you even if she wanted to."

"That makes me feel better. Hopefully she'll borrow a charger from someone and reach out to me."

"I hope so. The whole 'no cell phone' policy explains why frantic families aren't calling me, trying to find their loved ones," Cheryl said. "They aren't expecting to hear from them till Monday, which means they have no idea anything is even amiss."

"That's right."

"It doesn't really help us any though, does it?" Lacey asked. "And Roy, your grandma got on the bus after the phone collection had already happened."

"Maybe someone saw her with the phone and made her give it up?" Roy said. "Although I'm worried that even if she does find a charger, she's like me and has terrible service out here." Roy held up his phone. "I haven't had a consistent signal in a little while, and the farther down this road I go, the fewer bars I have."

"I totally am the same way," Lacey exclaimed. "I guess maybe there aren't many towers out here."

Cheryl nodded. "That's right. I had a hard time adjusting to that as well." She slowed the car down as she came upon a horse and buggy. "In fact, sometimes my phone doesn't even ring when I'm in certain locations. I'll get back to town and my phone will beep and let me know I have a voice mail."

"Yeah, that happened to me earlier too," Lacey agreed.

"Okay, this road is the only road between the Glicks' farm and the Millers' farm. The bus would've had to turn here because we know it didn't go straight."

"Let's drive down the road a bit. I'd like to just see if I notice anything out of the ordinary," Roy said. He fell silent for a few moments. "I just wish I could've gotten here sooner. I can't help but feel guilty."

Cheryl understood that sentiment. "I feel the same way. The tour was my idea in the first place. Now all those people are somewhere out there, including your grandma. And to top it off, I totally bought the lie that McGraw and Riggins told me. Otherwise, maybe the trail wouldn't be cold now."

"You can't blame yourself," Roy said. "Not one thing that happened yesterday was your fault. You never could have anticipated this." His face grew somber. "Believe me. I know something about blame. Most of my cases turn out okay. But sometimes...sometimes they don't. I had to learn early on in my career not to blame myself. Otherwise, I'd never be able to do what I do."

That made sense to Cheryl. Still though, she couldn't help but feel a little guilty. Maybe she should've left the tour business to Mean Richard. Then he'd be the one dealing with a missing busload of tourists. And an incognito pop star. The thought of Lacey tagging along with Richard made her smile a little.

"You can turn around now," Roy said. "I've seen enough."

The three of them rode back to the Swiss Miss in silence, and Cheryl couldn't help but notice that neither Lacey nor Roy offered any ideas about what to do next.

What she needed was a clue. Something that would help her figure out what the next step in finding the bus should be. Until then, she'd just pray.

Chapter Twelve

Naomi greeted them when they entered the store. "Did you learn anything new?"

"No, but I'm glad to have seen the route myself," Roy said. "I think perhaps the next step is to investigate everyone onboard the bus." He turned to Cheryl. "Can you give me a list of everyone? Names, addresses, phone numbers... whatever you may have from their registration form."

She nodded. "I can. Let me get that for you, and I'll be right back." She motioned around the store. "Feel free to look around while you wait."

"I'll show you around," Lacey said cheerfully. "Let me show you these cool dolls first."

Cheryl watched them walk off and felt a tiny pang of... jealousy? She hadn't been around many available men since she'd moved to Sugarcreek, not to mention that she'd spent the past several months trying to get over Lance. Roy didn't wear a wedding ring, and he was certainly attractive. Why hadn't she been the one to interact flirtatiously with him? Did that mean she wasn't as ready to jump into the dating pool as she thought she was? Or did it mean that her interest had already been captured by someone else? Someone a little more local than Roy. Someone who wore a hat and was named Levi...

"Here you go," she said a few minutes later as she handed Roy the list of names and information. "I think you'll find everything you need in there. Let me know if you need anything else, and I'll try to get it for you."

He smiled, and for the first time she noticed a tiny dimple in his right cheek. "Thank you. I'm going to start going through these names from my hotel room tonight. I'm staying at the Sugarcreek Village Inn. It's not far from here. I'll be back first thing in the morning to let you know if I've found anything of interest. Call me right away if anything develops."

"Oh, I will. I promise." She thought briefly of mentioning Michael to him. Maybe he was staying at the Village Inn too. It was one of the closest hotels to Sugarcreek's main drag. If Roy and Michael were staying at the same place, it might make it easier for her to get some inside information about him.

She decided against mentioning it though—she'd try to find out more about Michael herself. No need involving Roy. She watched him leave, first stopping to talk privately to Lacey. Had the two of them made plans? She could clearly see the spark of attraction between them.

"You look like you are far, far away," Naomi observed.

Cheryl felt her face flush. "It's nothing. I was just thinking about a few things."

Naomi gave her a knowing look. "It's like my daed always said, 'No time is lost waiting on God.'"

"Is that your way of saying everything happens in God's perfect timing? Because if it is, my dad used to say that too." Cheryl grinned, once again taken aback by how much she felt she had in common with Naomi. On the surface, they looked like opposites, but beneath the surface they were a lot alike.

"Ja." Naomi smiled and patted Cheryl's arm. "I know something of heartbreak. It takes time to get over it."

"That it does." Cheryl nodded.

The bell over the door jingled, and a familiar woman walked in. Her store-bought tan was more faded than it had been last week, but Cheryl still recognized her. Cheryl had tried a self-tanner once and had turned out looking like an Oompa Loompa, so she could commiserate with the woman's orange hue. "Velma, right?"

The woman nodded, her face brightening as Cheryl remembered her name. "Yes, how are you?"

I've lost a tour bus full of people and am beginning to question whether I'll ever find true love and happiness. "Okay, I guess. Can I help you with something?"

"I came back to see if you had more of that delicious jam."

Cheryl walked around the counter and stopped next to Velma at the shelf that contained a few jars of Naomi's jam. "Only a few jars. And some fresh loaves of bread too."

Velma beamed. "I'll take it all." She scooped the jars up in her arms and carried them to the counter.

"You must really love this stuff," Cheryl remarked. "Do you have a lot of kids at home to eat this?"

Velma's face fell. "No. Kids just weren't in the cards for us. It's just me and my husband. He loves it so much. And I also send some to our relatives."

"That's right. In California."

The sunny face was back. "I can't believe you remembered that. I'm sure there are people in and out of here all day long. I'm touched that you remember my name, much less our conversation."

Cheryl smiled at the woman. "Well, I enjoyed talking to you. Besides, I think you said you were a newcomer to the area. I am too." If Cheryl felt out of place sometimes in Sugarcreek, Velma must feel like a fish out of water.

"Thanks." Velma noticed a Live Like the Amish flier taped to the counter. "Oh, I remember hearing about this a while back. Do you think there will be another one?"

Cheryl frowned. "I guess we'll have to wait to read the reviews of this one before we decide." *Pretty sure being taken hostage on a tour bus in the middle of Amish country might not garner the best of reviews.*

"It sounds just delightful. I think some of my relatives should take part if you ever do it again." Velma took her bag with a grin. "I'm sure I'll see you later!" She headed out the door.

"I don't believe I've met her before," Naomi observed. "Although she looks familiar."

"She's been in a few times. I think she and her husband bought a house around here somewhere. They're originally from California though."

"I wonder what made them relocate here?"

Cheryl shrugged. "Who knows? Maybe peace and quiet? You know, the pace of life here is a little slower than a lot of places. Maybe she and her husband wanted to slow down."

"True. You know what they say, 'Life in the fast lane is normally a blur.'" Naomi grinned.

"Is that one from your dad too?"

Naomi shook her head. "That was some of my maam's advice when I was in rumspringa. She needn't have worried though. I love my life here in Sugarcreek. I meant it at lunch today. There's nowhere else I would rather be, and there never has been." Worry flashed across her pretty face, and Cheryl wondered if she was thinking about some of her own children. Her stepdaughter, Sarah, Seth's daughter with his first wife Ruth, had left the Amish faith to marry an Englischer. Ruth had died in childbirth with Sarah, so Naomi had been the only mother she'd ever known. Although Cheryl wasn't around when Sarah left, she'd recently gotten to know the girl when she'd come back to town over Christmas. It was difficult for Naomi and Seth not to have their daughter as a full-time part of the family.

And Esther was in rumspringa now, exploring the *Englisch* world to decide where she belonged. It must be so hard on Amish parents, waiting to see what their much-loved children would decide to do. Although in a way, their Englischer counterparts had to do the same thing. While Cheryl wasn't a parent, she could imagine how much worry and prayer was involved in raising a child. And once they reached a certain age and got to make their own decisions, it must be so hard to stand by and watch them make choices that led them far away from their upbringing.

"Well it's good advice." Cheryl looked at her watch. "I think perhaps we should go ahead and close up. The day has gotten away from me."

"And yet, I do not know if we are even one step closer to finding the bus."

"Let's just pray that Roy Neal finds something useful in the list of names. Maybe there is something we're missing."

Cheryl put the Closed sign in the window and locked the door behind them.

"We will see you in the morning," Naomi said. "I hope you can get some rest. Maybe tomorrow Roy will have good news for us."

Cheryl and Lacey nodded and said good-bye to Naomi and Esther.

"I like them," Lacey said once they'd parted ways. "I've never known any Amish people. They are just regular people."

Cheryl laughed. She'd thought the same thing when she'd first come to Sugarcreek. "Yep. I came to that same realization when I moved here. I realized that regardless of our backgrounds or lifestyles, there are certain commonalities we all seem to have."

"Like what?"

"A need to belong to something bigger than ourselves. A desire for friendship. A longing for love. I also think we're all created with a deep need for Jesus. Some people may not act on that, but it's there."

Lacey nodded. "I think you're right. On all counts."

"I need to swing by the Honey Bee Café for a few minutes. Do you want to go with me, or would you rather go on to Aunt Mitzi's cottage now?" Despite the missing bus, Cheryl hadn't forgotten her promise to Kathy. She wanted to check in and see how things were going with Heather and Michael.

"I'd like to go on to your aunt's cottage now if that's okay."

Cheryl nodded. "Of course. Do you want me to drive you, or do you want to walk?" Cheryl normally walked the short distance to the Swiss Miss, but she'd driven today since Lacey was here—and since she knew she'd need to have her car available in case there was news from the tour group.

"I'll walk. It will be nice to walk down the street without anyone knowing who I am." Lacey grinned and adjusted her *kapp*. "I'm just another Sugarcreek girl going home from work."

Cheryl laughed. "Have fun. The key is under the Welcome mat. If you're hungry, there's some of Naomi's homemade bread in the kitchen."

Lacey's face lit up. "Sounds divine. See ya." She turned and headed toward the cottage.

Cheryl watched her go. Indeed, to any passersby, she'd appear to be just another Sugarcreek girl, headed home from work. What a burden it would be to always be recognized. These few days in Sugarcreek must feel so peaceful for Lacey. As much as Cheryl had grumbled about having the girl on the tour and then as a guest in her home, she was glad to give her some much-needed peace.

She stepped inside the Honey Bee Café and inhaled. She never got tired of the welcoming aroma. The place was already closed, but Cheryl knew Kathy and a few of her employees would still be there.

Heather was behind the counter, cleaning the coffeemaker, a glum expression on her face. She looked up when Cheryl walked in. "Kathy's not here. She had to run a few errands, but she'll be back in a little while if you want to wait."

"Oh, that's fine. I was just going to chat with her for a few minutes." She watched Heather work for a moment. The woman might be standing in the Honey Bee Café, but her mind was a million miles away. "Is everything okay?" Cheryl asked. On the one hand, she hated to pry, but on the other...she might find out more about Michael and put Kathy's mind at ease. "You look like you just lost your best friend."

Heather managed a tiny smile. "I'm fine. Just a little confused." She shook her head. "I don't want to bore you though."

"I'm a pretty good listener. Go ahead and tell me what you're confused about if you want to." Cheryl didn't need to have psychic powers to know what was on Heather's mind. She'd had enough relationship problems to be able to spot one a mile away.

"You know that guy Michael?"

Cheryl nodded.

"We went out last night, and I thought it was going to be a date—you know, dinner and maybe a movie or something. But instead, he just wanted to drive around and look at all these Amish homes and ask me questions about how they cook and do laundry and stuff." She frowned. "I don't think he asked me anything at all about myself. And I didn't learn much about him either."

Didn't sound like much of a date. "So what else did you guys talk about?"

Heather wrinkled her nose. "Mainly about what life's like here in Sugarcreek. He asked me if I had any Amish relatives or if I used to be Amish. It was so weird. Then he wanted to know about the café and if we had any Amish customers."

So Michael was fixated on the Amish for some reason? Was that his reason for visiting? "Did he tell you why he was in town?" Cheryl asked.

Heather shook her head. "He just said he was here on a working vacation. But he didn't say what kind of work." She sighed. "The weird thing is that you just missed him. He came by just a few minutes ago to tell me what a great time he had last night and to see if I wanted to do something again tonight."

"And?"

Heather grimaced. "I know I should've said no thanks, especially since he treated me more like a tour guide than a date, but I hated to turn him down. Maybe he was just nervous or something last night. Tonight we're going to Beachy's for dinner. Maybe we'll actually have a conversation then."

Cheryl wanted to believe that Michael was a good guy, even if just for Heather's sake, but her instincts told her that he wasn't taking the girl to dinner for the right reasons. Maybe if she could find out what type of business he was in, she'd have her answers. "I hope it goes well." She smiled. "Are you working tomorrow?"

Heather nodded. "Saturday mornings are one of our busiest. I'll be here."

"Have fun tonight, and tell Kathy I stopped by. I'll drop in tomorrow to visit with her."

Heather smiled. "Thanks, Cheryl. It was nice talking to you." She returned to her cleanup work.

Cheryl shivered as she ran to the car. The sun had barely gone down, and the temperature had dropped. She wondered again how the tour group was doing. Were they someplace warm? She hated not knowing.

When she arrived at the cottage, the place was dark. Had Lacey gone out? She unlocked the door and stepped inside. "Lacey?"

"I'm in here." A muffled voice came from the coat closet.

Cheryl flung open the door and found Lacey and Beau huddled together in the bottom of the closet, covered by a plaid throw. "What are you doing in there?"

Lacey crawled out of the closet. "Were they still outside? Did you see them?"

"What are you talking about?"

"Those men. The white car from yesterday." Lacey's face was devoid of color, and her voice shook.

"What about them?"

"I decided to walk around the block before I came here. As I was walking, I heard a car behind me. I glanced over my shoulder and saw them—going slow like they were following me. I know it was the same white car that followed us yesterday."

"Did they follow you all the way here?" Surely Lacey hadn't led them right to the place she was staying.

She shook her head. "I went the other direction. I ran to that little ice cream place and thankfully there was a whole group of Amish girls in there. When they left, I left and walked like I was part of their group." She managed a tiny grin. "I saw that work in a movie once. And it worked for me too. I didn't see the car when we came out of the shop, but even if they'd been out there, I don't think they would've noticed me."

Score one for ingenuity. "That was smart."

"And people say television kills brain cells." Lacey flopped down on the couch, and Beau jumped into her lap. "Once I felt like the coast was clear, I ran here. Thankfully I'm not too out of shape, even though I've ignored my workouts over the past couple of days."

"I think it probably takes more than two days to fall out of shape. I'd say you at least have until Tuesday." Cheryl tried to tease some of the stress out of Lacey, but it didn't appear to work.

"I felt so vulnerable." Lacey wrapped her arms around herself. "What if one of them had grabbed me and thrown me into the car?"

"Valid concern." Cheryl raked her fingers through her hair. It was hard to know how seriously to take Lacey's fear. Were the men dangerous or just paparazzi looking for a story? Or neither? "Did they say anything to you out the window? Or act as if they were going to get out and grab you?"

Lacey shook her head. "No. But still. I think not knowing their intentions makes it even scarier. If I knew what I was dealing with, I could be more prepared. But for months I've received these vague messages and now as soon as I get away from my normal life, I'm being followed. Something is going on. I definitely don't think they were just following some Amish girl home from work. I think they knew it was me."

Cheryl frowned. "And you're sure it was the same white car as yesterday?"

Lacey nodded. "I'm positive."

"I guess it's simple then. Find the car, find the men. Then once and for all, we'll be able to unmask your stalker and put your mind at ease."

Lacey smiled for the first time since Cheryl had arrived home. "It would be wonderful to rest easy again."

Cheryl's to-do list seemed overwhelming: find a bus full of missing tourists, find out if Michael was a bad guy, and now figure out who was following Lacey. She flipped through the mail until she came to a letter with Aunt Mitzi's scrawling handwriting.

She sank into her recliner and opened her aunt's letter, grateful for a bright spot in an otherwise tedious day.

Chapter Thirteen

Darling Cheryl,

I hope this letter finds you well. I realize it's entirely possible that we've spoken via e-mail or Skype recently, so this news could be old. I'm hopeful that the novelty of getting a handwritten letter will make up for that though.

By my calculations, your Live Like the Amish Tour should be just about to begin, or perhaps you're right in the midst of it. Either way, I hope things are going well. I think it seems like a delightful time, and I feel sure your guests will go home with memorable experiences. Remember that the biggest thing they are looking for is more than likely a connection to the past. Among those of an older generation, their lives weren't that different than the Amish lifestyle today (electricity notwithstanding). They were connected to their families and communities far more than they were the outside world. They cooked meals from scratch and spent summer evenings churning ice cream on the front porch. I feel certain that your tour will transport the group to a simpler way of life they will enjoy.

Of course, then they'll want their phones so they can post about the experience on Facebook!

As for me, things here have been interesting lately. There are two college girls here from the States who've come to do a month-long missionary shadowing program. At first I questioned why I'd ever agreed to such a thing. You should've seen them when they arrived! Full makeup, perfect hair, immaculate clothes. Not exactly what I'm used to seeing these days.

But Cheryl, once they were settled in and after they'd passed the "selfie with every new thing" stage, they have turned out to be wonderful helpers. Their hearts are definitely in the right place. Kimmie is tireless with the children, and they adore her. Crystal has a heart for teens, and she's made great strides with them in spite of language and cultural barriers. I admit to you that I feel a little ashamed. I was too quick to judge.

Let that be a lesson for us all! You never know someone's heart until you give them a chance.

I can't wait to hear all about your adventures with the tour group. Give Naomi and her sweet family my best.

I love you,
Aunt Mitzi

Cheryl leaned her head against the recliner and closed her eyes. As usual, Aunt Mitzi was right on the mark. How often had Cheryl been guilty of judging someone before she'd put herself in their shoes? Lacey was a prime example. In spite of her fame and regardless of the fact that she was sometimes self-absorbed, she wasn't at all what Cheryl had expected.

Today she'd seen her interact with a few customers in the store, and her demeanor hadn't been that of someone who thought themselves better than others. Instead she'd been kind and open, quick to smile and laugh with the customers.

Granted, she'd been wearing a disguise, and for all Cheryl knew, her kind-spirited ways could've been an act, but Cheryl didn't think so. Instead she wondered if the girl had been portrayed unfairly in the media and Cheryl had automatically believed what she'd been led to believe instead of offering the benefit of the doubt that Lacey deserved.

A lesson for all indeed.

"Everything okay?" Lacey asked.

Cheryl jumped. She was so used to being alone in the house, she'd forgotten Lacey was sitting on the couch. "Just reading a letter from Aunt Mitzi." She grinned. "You were so quiet over there, I'd forgotten you were in the room."

Lacey turned the television on and began flipping through the channels. "I guess I was just thinking about some stuff." She stopped flipping and stared at the TV screen. "Check this out."

"In breaking news," the perky brunette host said, "we're getting reports that pop superstar Lacey Landers has been spotted in Ohio's Amish country."

Lacey gasped as her picture flashed on the screen.

"While the news hasn't been confirmed, speculation is that Miss Landers could be there researching her upcoming film role in which she'll portray a young Amish widow." The entertainment host flashed a devious smile at the camera. "I'm not sure how believable she will be in that role, but I do believe that with Lacey's checkered past and her recent run-ins with paparazzi—not to mention the rumor of a persistent stalker...her whereabouts won't stay a secret for long."

Lacey flipped off the TV and tossed the remote on the couch next to her, causing Beau to wake up from one of his many naps. "It just makes me so mad," she said finally.

"How could they possibly know you're here?" Cheryl wondered out loud. "You're sure you didn't tell anyone?"

Lacey shook her head. "No one. Not even my dog sitter." She sighed. "Only Blake knows. I changed into my disguise when I arrived at the airport in Ohio. No one even suspected. I got on the waiting bus and none of the people on there even batted an eye at me."

"Did you post that cuckoo clock selfie? Because that's kind of a landmark here in Sugarcreek."

"Of course not. I took the photo to post later once I'm gone from here. I rarely ever post photos of myself in certain locations anymore. Not since that guy has been trying to get in touch with me. I'm always afraid he'll see the post and come find me."

That was understandable. And smart. "Well, at this point they're only saying it's a rumor. And she mentioned nothing about your being disguised. So if they're here, maybe they are looking for everyday Lacey and not Amish or elderly Lacey. Do you really think those guys in the white car are photographers?"

"Who else would they be? Unless the guy who has been trying to contact me has somehow figured out I'm here." Lacey's face grew white. "I think I'd take the paparazzi over that." She sighed. "The only thing I can think of is Riggins and McGraw—or whoever they are. They know I'm here. Maybe they leaked it."

"True. But they seemed so set on finding that bus, that surely they wouldn't take the time to tip off a reporter."

"Let's hope not." Lacey's phone buzzed. She held it up. "Blake. I'm sure he's going to try to convince me to get on a plane." She left the room to take the call.

Cheryl considered Lacey's life for a moment. Was fame worth the constant invasion of privacy? She'd often wondered that as she'd seen details and photos of famous peoples' private lives splashed across magazines and Web sites.

Lacey returned, grumbling under her breath. "I know him well. When I declined the plane, he wanted to send a bodyguard. Can you picture that? An Amish girl strolling down the streets of Sugarcreek with a big burly bodyguard following her?"

Cheryl had to smile at the image. "So why stay? You can go back to your life, and we'll figure out the bus thing. In fact, once your bag is recovered, I can just send it to you."

Lacey's eyes filled with tears. "It's not about the bag. Or really even about the bus at this point." She tucked a strand of hair behind her ear. "These past two days are the most normal my life has been in years." She let out a laugh. "Can you imagine? A disappearing bus and fake detectives and some car following me—and yet it's the most normal I've felt in a long time."

"What do you mean?"

"I can't get a cup of coffee without a picture of it being online. Then once the photo is posted, an army of people share their opinions about how I look, discuss whether I've gained weight, speculate that I'm a diva to work with...stuff like that. People hide behind the anonymity of the Internet to say some pretty heinous stuff. And they may think that because I'm famous, it doesn't matter to me." She shrugged. "But words hurt, no matter who you are."

"I can't even imagine." Just like Aunt Mitzi and the college interns, Cheryl had been too quick to judge Lacey. She was a genuinely nice girl with a good heart. "So why keep going? The tour, the movies? Why do it?"

Lacey smiled. "It's what I love to do. The creativity, the craft. It's hard work. I rehearse long hours. I appreciate working hard and seeing it pay off. And I know the trade-off is that I can't have a normal life." She picked up the prayer kapp she'd worn over her bun. "That's why I want to stay a little while longer. Just like today, talking to Roy... I haven't been able to talk to a guy like that in a long time. These days I have to worry if the guy likes me or if they hope I can help them career-wise. Today I was just me. I wasn't the pop star or the movie star. I was just a girl talking to a guy about his grandmother and showing him what an Amish-made doll looks like."

"I guess I can understand that." Cheryl smiled. "Well, you're welcome to stay here. You are actually good at coming up with ideas about the missing bus. Maybe you can stay till it's found."

"Oh, I hope so. This is their second night staying wherever they are. It's so weird to think about, isn't it? Like, are they still on the bus? Are they at a hotel? I mean, it seems like when they didn't stop at the farm, they would've all been really upset."

Cheryl had actually been trying not to think about it.

The phone next to her rang, startling both women and sending Beau flying out of the room.

Cheryl picked it up and locked eyes with Lacey. "It's the Troyers' number again."

Chapter Fourteen

Cheryl's hand trembled a bit as she raised the phone to her ear. "Hello," she said.

"Everyone is safe for now." The muffled voice wasted no time getting to the point of the call.

"Where are they?" Cheryl asked. But it was no use. The caller had already hung up.

She relayed the message to Lacey.

"It's so weird."

"Do you think he's telling the truth?"

Cheryl shrugged. "This is my first experience with this sort of thing. I can only assume he is. Otherwise why go to the trouble to reach out to me?"

"True."

"I guess I'd better call Roy." Cheryl eyed Lacey. "Unless you'd rather do it."

Lacey beamed. "Oh yeah. I totally would." She took the business card from Cheryl's outstretched hand then looked unsure. "Do you really think it's okay?"

"Sure."

Lacey managed a tiny smile. "I'm nervous. I don't remember the last time I called a guy. I mean, I know I have a reason, but at the same time it feels so transparent."

"Would you rather me just do it?" Cheryl asked.

Lacey shook her head. "I'd like to talk to him, but the thought of dialing that number makes me all woozy."

Cheryl laughed. "Come on. You're Lacey Landers. You sell out stadiums, and your face is on magazine covers. Believe me, *he's* probably going to be the nervous one."

"You think?"

"I do. Call him from your room," Cheryl said. "That way you'll have a little privacy. If he has any news, just let me know before you go to bed. I'm going to bed soon, but I'll be up reading for a little while."

Lacey smiled. "Thanks. I'll let you know if he has news." She practically floated to the guest room.

Cheryl watched her go, remembering what it was like to feel giddy over a phone call. Would she experience such a thing again? She knew in her heart that Naomi was right. Everything in life was all about God's timing. She could clearly see the path she'd taken to get where she was today and how His hand had been guiding her all along. The disappointment and heartbreak over Lance, coupled with Aunt Mitzi's opportunity to pursue her lifelong dream of mission work had worked together to lead Cheryl to Sugarcreek. And she had no doubt this was where she was supposed to be.

So maybe patience was the key after all. And in the meantime, she'd enjoy the friendships she'd established since moving to Sugarcreek. Her mind drifted to Kathy Snyder. She and Kathy had formed a friendship in the months Cheryl had been in Sugarcreek, and she appreciated Kathy's concern over Heather, but she felt like she wasn't making much progress in learning about Michael. She dialed Kathy's number.

"Cheryl, I was hoping you'd call," Kathy said. "Heather said you stopped by."

"I did." Cheryl curled her feet underneath her in the recliner. Her momma used to tell her she looked like a pretzel when she sat like that, but it sure was comfortable. "I heard about Heather's date last night."

Kathy laughed. "Poor girl. She's so confused. And frankly, so am I. Did she tell you some of the questions he asked her?"

"Nothing specific. Just stuff about Amish life and farms. Did she give you more specifics than that?"

"Apparently he had a list of questions. I mean, not a literal list, but he was just overly curious. He wanted to know all about gas-operated light fixtures in Amish homes and what the rules are as far as riding in a buggy versus hiring a driver. They were very specific questions."

"I appreciate learning about a new way of life, but it kind of sounds like he has an agenda."

Kathy sighed heavily. "That's exactly what I thought. But what? At this point, I'm not sure the danger is that this guy Michael is going to break Heather's heart. It's more…what is he really up to?"

"Your guess is as good as mine." Cheryl hadn't been able to get a good read on Michael yesterday at the Honey Bee, but she was pretty sure he was hiding something.

"Thanks for your help with this. I am at least feeling better now that I know my instincts were right about him. Something doesn't add up, but I'm not totally sure what that is."

So many things these days didn't. Cheryl took a breath. Now that Riggins and McGraw had been outed as bogus detectives, she didn't have to abide by their plea to keep the missing bus a secret. "I have news," she said quietly. She filled Kathy in on the events of the last day.

"Oh my!" Kathy exclaimed. "Here I've been going on and on about Heather and her love problems and you've been dealing with something so huge."

Cheryl laughed. "Well, there's no way you could've guessed something like that. I'm still sort of in shock over the whole thing. I halfway expect some hidden camera host to jump out and tell me I've been the victim of a big prank." She sighed. "Except that there's more to the story than just the missing bus." She explained about Roy Neal and his grandmother. "He's a legit FBI agent. And his concern over his grandma is real. So I'm pretty sure this whole thing is really happening."

"Is there anything I can do to help?" Kathy asked.

"Pray. That's the best thing at this point. And if you see Mickey Simmons around town, call me right away."

"The group came by the Honey Bee yesterday, right?"

"Sure did. I've already talked to Heather about it. She was the one who waited on them."

"And she didn't notice anything odd?" Kathy asked.

"Nope. Mickey got a phone call and had an argument with whoever it was, but I guess that's not odd."

"I only stepped out of my office for a few minutes. I sure wish I could give you some helpful information, but it seemed like a normal tour group to me."

"Except that after they left your place, they disappeared."

Kathy let out a low whistle. "Maybe this whole thing will make sense soon. In the meantime, I'll be praying for their safety. And your sanity."

Cheryl laughed. "Thanks."

She clicked off the phone and headed for the kitchen. She put some strawberry jam on the last two slices of Naomi's homemade bread and settled at the table. It appeared that Lacey had eaten already, so she didn't interrupt her phone call. She could hear the low murmurings of her voice from the guest room.

Once she'd straightened up the kitchen, she headed for bed.

Lacey's laughter drifted through the door as Cheryl passed the guest room. Surely if she had anything important to report from Roy, she would've done so by now. Cheryl scooted Beau over from his spot in the middle of the bed and climbed underneath the covers. Tomorrow was Saturday. Typically it was a busy day at the Swiss Miss. She'd already scheduled both Esther and her friend Lydia to work shifts tomorrow, in anticipation of her being busy with the Live Like the Amish tour.

Instead, it looked like she'd be busy tomorrow trying to *find* the Live Like the Amish tour.

Chapter Fifteen

The next morning, Cheryl gently rapped on Lacey's door. She was already dressed and ready for the day, but so far she hadn't heard a peep from Lacey.

Finally, the door opened and a bleary-eyed Lacey stood grinning. "I overslept. So sorry. It won't take me long to get ready."

"Up late?" Cheryl asked.

Lacey nodded. "I guess we had a lot to talk about. He's a very interesting guy."

"I'll bet."

"The reason it took him so long to get here is because he was at some secluded little resort somewhere in Canada. He said just finding the transportation to get him to Sugarcreek as fast as he did was a challenge. He really feels badly though and is so determined to find his grandma today."

"I hope he does." Cheryl lifted her coffee mug. "Do you want anything to eat? If we leave quickly we can stop by the Swiss Village Market and pick up some pastries. You might even want to sample a fry pie for breakfast."

"That sounds perfect. I'll hurry."

Twenty minutes later they pulled into the parking lot at Swiss Village Market. "This is a great little store," Cheryl said. "It's kind of a combination gift shop and grocery store depending on which side you enter. They have these variety samplers of cheese bits that are wonderful. I stopped in right after I arrived in Sugarcreek and was pretty much hooked."

Lacey chose fry pies in two flavors—strawberry and grape—and came away with a bag of cheese as well. "Blake would just die if he saw me eating this." She grinned. "And you know what? I don't even care."

Cheryl put her sole purchase—a pineapple fry pie—on the conveyer belt at the checkout. "I would happily eat these every day, except that I'm in a constant battle with my weight."

Lacey rolled her eyes. "You look normal. Not like me, with every bone sticking out. I have seriously got the worst case of chicken legs you've ever seen." She collected her bag from the cashier.

"Does the camera really add ten pounds?" Cheryl asked once they were outside. She'd always heard that it did.

"Oh, definitely."

"All the more reason I won't be headed to Hollywood." Cheryl tried to make light of it, but she really did need to lose a few pounds. Now that she was thirty, it wasn't as easy as it used to be to keep the pounds off. And especially in Sugarcreek, surrounded by delicious and rich food, she was more self-conscious about it than she used to be.

Lacey glanced around the parking lot.

"Everything okay?"

She shrugged. "Just looking for that white car. I keep expecting them to pop up again."

"Let's hope they're sleeping in today." Cheryl still didn't know what to make of the men in the car.

Once they were safely in the car, Lacey bit into a strawberry fry pie. "Oh, wow. This is so good."

"Told you." Cheryl grinned.

"It's worth the extra pounds," Lacey said once she finished her pie. "I'm kinda tempted to eat the other one, but I'll save that for a midmorning snack."

Her cell phone buzzed in her lap. "Ugh," she groaned.

"Trouble?" Cheryl glanced over at her.

"Just Blake. Checking in on me today. Reminding me to work out. Same old stuff." She sighed.

They got out of the car and walked toward the Swiss Miss. Cheryl still couldn't get used to driving to work, but with Lacey as her guest and all the chaos of the missing bus, it just made more sense. "Sorry."

"He's always looking out for me. I owe a lot of my career to him. But sometimes I want a little more freedom." She held up her remaining fry pie. "I shouldn't have to feel guilty for indulging every now and then, but somehow I do. And his 'be sure to work out' texts don't help."

Cheryl couldn't imagine someone else having that kind of input in her life. She sensed a subject change was in order. "I'm really hoping Roy has some good news for us today. Did he mention last night if he'd found anything interesting on the list of tour attendees?"

The mention of Roy brought a smile to Lacey's face. "Nope. He mostly just talked about how guilty he felt about taking so long to get here. He did say there was a senator's grandfather on the bus, but he didn't really seem to think that had anything to do with the bus disappearing."

They were in view of the Swiss Miss. "Looks like you've already received a package today," Lacey said. "I didn't realize any delivery services ran this early."

Cheryl knelt down to take a look at the package. "There's no address label. This must've been left here for me." She lifted it and handed it to Lacey. "Hold it while I unlock the door."

Once they were inside, they took the box directly to the back. Cheryl pulled some scissors out of a drawer and used them to cut the packing tape that held the box closed.

"No way!" Lacey exclaimed. "It's my bag from the bus." She reached for the bag, but Cheryl grabbed her arm.

"Wait. I think we should call Roy first. Don't touch it in case there are fingerprints or something. I feel like that's what they would do on TV."

Lacey nodded. "You're right. That's exactly what I did in my TV movie, *Murder, She Blogged*. I'll call him now."

Cheryl busied herself with the necessary steps needed to open the store, but her mind was churning. Who had left the bag on the steps? And why? She wondered again about the strange phone calls and how they figured in.

"Roy is on his way," Lacey said once she'd hung up. "He's hoping this is the break we need. So far, the list hasn't given him any leads."

Ten minutes later, Roy walked in, his hair still damp from the shower. He stifled a yawn.

Cheryl bit back a remark about late nights and puppy love. Maybe it was best to keep the actual FBI agent on her side.

"Any idea who may have left the box here?" Roy asked.

Cheryl shook her head. "No. It was here when we arrived. I thought I might visit a couple of the businesses nearby to see if any of the owners happened to see anyone carrying a box this morning. Or even saw anyone out of the ordinary this early."

"I'll leave you to do that," Roy said. "In the meantime, I'll take the packaging and see if I can get any prints from it." He looked in the box at Lacey's bag. "But first, let's go ahead and remove the bag."

"Do you want me to do that?" Lacey asked.

He nodded. "Take the bag out and pour out the contents. I want to know if there's anything missing."

Lacey lifted her bag, a giant hobo style in a blue and white chevron print, and slowly emptied it on to the table. She began pilfering through her things then stopped. "It kind of reminds me of that magazine that does that whole 'what's in your bag' feature. They asked me to participate. Maybe I should just take a photo of all this stuff."

Roy smiled at her. "For now just look through and tell me if there's anything missing. Or anything unusual."

Were ten different lipstick shades unusual? They would be for Cheryl. "Did you have anything valuable in the bag?"

Lacey gave her a look. "The *bag* is valuable. I meant it when I said it was a one of a kind. But there doesn't seem to be anything missing." She riffled through the piles of makeup, ponytail holders, and ink pens and plucked out a piece of paper. "Hold up. This wasn't there before."

"How do you know? My purse is full of receipts and things. If someone added ten scraps of paper, I'd never know it." Cheryl knew that organization wasn't her strong point. There was no telling how much time she'd have to spend searching through her own purse for a particular receipt. And to know there'd been one added—she had to admit she was impressed.

"I scan all my receipts with an app on my phone and then throw them away. I hate having all that paper in my purse. It bugs me."

Cheryl eyed the loot on the table. Sure enough, there was no other paper among her things. "What is it?"

"A receipt from Swiss Village Market." Lacey looked up. "That's where we went this morning, but that was the first time I'd been there. This is definitely not mine." She turned it over. "Someone wrote on the back. It says, 'The time to make friends is before you need them.'"

"That's odd," Roy mused.

"I think that's an Amish proverb. I have a book of them at home, and I'm pretty sure I've read it before. I wonder if that's intentional." Cheryl couldn't imagine what the phrase was supposed to mean to them.

"What is the receipt for?" Roy asked.

Lacey turned the receipt back over and squinted at the faded words. "Looks like someone bought twelve smoky cheese samplers and twelve regular cheese samplers. It was bought on Thursday at 11:38 a.m."

"From what you said, that's around the same time the tour group was in your store," Roy said, glancing at Cheryl.

She nodded. "It is almost exactly the time they were here. I remember looking at the clock at 11:40. And you want to know something else odd? Twelve smoky cheese samplers and twelve regular cheese samplers equals twenty-four. That's the number of people onboard the bus."

"So...someone bought cheese for the group? And put the receipt in Lacey's bag?" Roy frowned. "And then wrote some random Amish proverb on it?"

"It seems like someone is trying to tell us something," Cheryl said. "But I'm not totally sure what."

"Maybe it's supposed to be proof that the people aren't dead or anything," Lacey piped up.

Cheryl and Roy both looked at her.

She blushed. "I just mean that if whoever took them was going to kill them, they probably wouldn't buy them cheese first, now would they?"

She had a point. An odd point, but a point nonetheless.

"What are your plans for the day?" Cheryl asked. "Do you have any leads?"

Roy looked sheepish. "Well, now I do." He held up the box. "I'll take this and see if it gives me anything useful. Other than that, I'm back to square one. I've alerted the surrounding towns and given them Mickey's description, as well as the license number on the bus. I'm hoping that will turn up something new."

"Good." Cheryl nodded. Now that McGraw and Riggins were out of the picture, she was happy to have as much help as possible in finding the bus. "Will it be on the news? I'm worried about the families of the group finding out. Do you think I should call them?"

Roy shook his head. "At this point, we're doing everything that needs to be done. I don't think creating a media frenzy is a good idea. It may make the situation worse." He frowned. "I'm getting pressure though. I've asked for a little more time, and if I can uncover a new lead, it will buy me even more time. The last thing I need is a bunch of reporters camped out here. For some reason, anything that happens in Amish country that's the least bit out of the ordinary attracts a big following."

Cheryl nodded.

"How about you ladies?" Roy asked. "You're going to visit around and see if anyone happened to see the mystery delivery person?"

"Right."

"Um." Lacey looked uncertain. "I know this isn't related to the bus or anything, but I'd really like to go visit my nana today. I can take a cab or whatever though."

Cheryl shook her head. "I'll drive you. We can head there once we're done checking around about the package."

Lacey smiled. "Thank you."

Just as they were saying good-bye to Roy, Naomi and Esther arrived.

"Ladies," he said, nodding at them. "I'll be back once I have some information." He reached the door then stopped and turned back around. "Oh, Cheryl. I forgot one thing."

Something in his voice made her leery. "What's that?"

"Chief Twitchell will be tracking you down sometime today. I've explained the situation to him, but he may be a little irritable that you didn't call him right away."

She wrinkled her nose. Great. An irritable Twitchell was just what she needed to make her day complete. "Thanks for the heads-up."

He hesitated.

"Is there something else?"

Roy nodded. "Well, yeah. Chief Twitchell mentioned that you had a habit of getting involved in things that he thinks should be left to his office."

She and Naomi exchanged a knowing glance. "I wouldn't call it a habit. But there have been a few times where Naomi and I have had sort of an inside track into whatever was going on. I would think that Chief Twitchell would be happy for the assistance."

Roy's blue eyes twinkled. "I'm not sure *happy* is the word I'd use."

"Yeah, probably not," Cheryl agreed.

Once Roy had gone to check on fingerprints, Cheryl was ready to do a little investigating of her own, regardless of what Twitchell thought. "Who wants to go with me? I'm going to stop by the Honey Bee Café to see if anyone there saw someone carrying a box early this morning. If not, I'll move on to a couple of the other stores in the area. Surely someone saw something."

"If not, what will we do?" Lacey asked.

Cheryl shrugged. "Let's cross that bridge when we get there. I'm hoping someone around here saw something out of the ordinary this morning."

"I'll stay here with Esther in case it gets busy," Naomi said. "Lydia won't be in for another hour."

"Thanks, Naomi. We'll check back in with you before we head to the retirement home to see Lacey's grandparents."

Naomi nodded.

Cheryl said a silent prayer that today would bring them the break they needed to figure out the bus's whereabouts. And if not, that at least the tour goers were as safe as the mystery caller wanted her to think.

Chapter Sixteen

Cheryl and Lacey walked the short distance to the Honey Bee Café. It was one of Cheryl's favorite places for lunch near the store. She loved that she could walk there, but even more than that she loved the inviting atmosphere of the place. It was the perfect place to get a cup of coffee too. "One of my favorite things is the honeycomb-flavored coffee. It's so yummy." They climbed the steps to the café. "And the soups. There's nothing I love better on a cold day than soup for lunch."

"That sounds really good." Lacey grinned. "It's crazy. I ate breakfast not long ago and now you're making my stomach growl with all this talk about food." She held up her phone. "And now that I've confessed that, I expect a 'work out' text from Blake at any time. Sometimes I think he has a bug on me."

Heather greeted Cheryl with a smile. She seemed much happier than she had been the day before. "Honeycomb coffee?" she asked.

Cheryl smiled. It was nice when someone remembered her usual order. She shook her head. "Not today. Actually I wondered if anyone happened to see anything unusual this morning near the Swiss Miss."

Heather wrinkled her nose. "What do you mean?"

"When you were coming to work this morning, did you happen to see anyone carrying a box anywhere near the store?"

She shook her head. "Hang on. Let me see if Bella happened to see anything." She stepped into the kitchen.

"Looks like we may strike out," Lacey whispered.

A minute later, she returned. "Bella is in the middle of baking right now, but she says to tell you that she saw someone carrying a box. At least she thinks so. But she doesn't know who it was. She didn't pay that much attention, but she thinks it was around six this morning because she was driving to work." She shrugged an apology. "Sorry we aren't more help."

"That's okay. At least it's a start. We have a time frame. I can check around at a few other places to see if anyone else saw someone."

Heather smiled. "Okay, good."

"Do I detect a little more happiness than I did yesterday?" Cheryl asked. "And does that mean dinner at Beachy's went well?"

Heather's cheeks turned pink. "I guess. I mean, at least this time he didn't just ask stuff about Amish people."

"So does that mean the two of you had a real conversation where you learned more about one another?"

Heather frowned. "He learned more about me. But I can't really say the same." She sighed. "Maybe there's something wrong with me. Dating seems harder for me than for other people."

Lacey patted her hand on the counter. "I doubt it. I think it's hard for everyone." She shook her head. "At least I know for me it is. I must've had like a billion bad dates in my life."

Heather stared at her with wide eyes. Clearly the idea of an Amish girl having had a billion dates was too much for her to handle.

Lacey removed her hand from the counter. She sent a sheepish smile in Heather's direction. "But what do I know?"

Cheryl fought back laughter. "I suspect we've all had our share of bad dates." She turned to Lacey. "Are you ready? We'd better get going. We have a lot to accomplish today."

Lacey nodded.

"Heather, I hope you continue to have a good day."

Heather grinned. "I have another date tonight. This time we're going to check out a few of the sites that have been in some of those movies that filmed here. Michael really wants to see some of the locations."

Cheryl didn't point out how odd that seemed. Maybe she and Kathy were just looking for a reason not to trust the guy though. "Hope to see you at church tomorrow." Cheryl and Heather both attended the local Silo Church which wasn't really the church name but a reference to the big silo that stood near the entrance. Although the silo was no longer in use, the church kept it on the grounds. It made a great landmark and was easy to give directions to. Cheryl had been delighted to find a church home full of love and grace. She wondered if Lacey would attend with her tomorrow. They hadn't discussed it yet.

"Oh, definitely. I'll be there." Heather waved good-bye to them as they left.

"So that was kind of another dead end," Lacey observed as they walked across the street to the Swiss Miss.

"Pretty much." Cheryl sighed. "We can't catch a break."

When they entered the store, Esther was waiting on a customer. They waved to her and went to the back where Naomi sat, concentrating on a sheet of paper. "Are you working on something?" Cheryl asked.

Naomi jumped. "Oh! You startled me." She smiled. "I'm just making a list of what all has happened these past couple of days. I thought I would see if anything jumped out at me."

"That's a good idea. Did you come up with anything?"

"Maybe." She tapped the paper with her pencil. "Are you up for a little trip after a while?"

Cheryl sat down. "Sure. Where to?"

"Well, I have been trying to think about the parts of this puzzle that do not seem to fit." She looked at Cheryl. "What do we know so far to be true?"

"Lacey missed the bus. Roy's granny was being chased by some men. The bus made two stops after it left here, and then it disappeared." Cheryl ticked them off on her fingers. "Someone seems to be leaving us clues. Mickey's cell phone is going to voice mail."

Their eyes met. "Mickey," Cheryl said.

"He is the part that does not fit. Where is he? Did someone force him to drive somewhere else? Is he okay?" Naomi wrote his name on the paper. "If we find Mickey, we find the bus."

"So we should go visit his place."

Naomi nodded. "This time we need to do more than just drive by."

"Sounds like a plan. We'll go as soon as Lacey and I get back from visiting her grandparents."

"Um. I don't think I'm gonna go to the bus driver's house. Is that okay?" Lacey asked. She'd been sitting in the corner furiously texting while Cheryl and Naomi talked. She was so quiet for once, Cheryl had almost forgotten she was there.

"Sure. Do you want me to just take you back to my house when we get back?" Cheryl asked. "Or you're welcome to stay at the store if you'd rather."

"Actually Roy is going to come pick me up." She blushed. "We're going to have a late lunch." She smoothed her simple Amish dress then looked at Naomi with concern. "Will that be okay? If people see me out in public with Roy, I mean? Will they think I'm doing something wrong?" She frowned. "I don't want to do anything that will make a bad impression or make people uncomfortable."

"You look young enough, I believe people may just think you are in rumspringa." Naomi smiled. "But it is nice of you to be concerned. Remember though that we can be friends with Englischers if we want to. It is likely that the only people who would bat an eye would be tourists who might be shocked to see you on a date with someone who is clearly not Amish."

"Will you be gone long?" Cheryl asked. She cringed. Her question came off sounding like a mom. Lacey wasn't that much younger than she was. "I mean, do you want me to give you a house key or leave it unlocked if I go somewhere?"

Lacey giggled. "Chill. It's just lunch. We may go drive along the route we think the bus took, just to see if we see anything. He mentioned going to some of the hotels and describing Riggins and McGraw to see if anyone has seen them around. Hopefully they've left by now, but you never know. They could still be lurking."

"Sounds like fun." She turned her attention back to Naomi. "We'll be back in a bit."

Lacey nodded. "We won't stay long today. I know you ladies have things to do."

Not to mention that she had a lunch date.

Cheryl and Lacey headed to the car and made the short drive to Dover.

"Do you think you should call ahead and tell them you're coming?" Cheryl asked. "Or at least warn them that you're in disguise?"

"It won't matter much," Lacey said. "Nana is legally blind. My papa can't see that well either, if he's even awake." She shook her head. "My disguise won't even phase them. Plus the less people who know, the better. You never know when an aide or nurse could be in the room, so I definitely don't want to call and tell them I'm coming. Then there'd be people curious about me stopping in, and I really would like to just have a low-key visit."

Cheryl understood. "Okay." She slowed the vehicle as they arrived in the Dover city limits. "What's the name of the place again?"

"Shady Acres. It's just up here on the right. You should see the sign out front."

Cheryl flipped on her blinker as she spotted the sign. "And it's a retirement community?"

"One section is a nursing home and the other is more of a come-and-go type of place. That's what Nana and Papa are in. They don't need full-time medical care as much as they just need some assistance. This way, someone cooks their meals, makes sure they take their meds...stuff like that. But the facility is really nice and they have lots of activities for them to do if they want to—or they can just do their own thing." She unbuckled her seat belt. "I helped them choose the place a couple of years ago. When Nana's eyesight started to fail, it was time for them to move somewhere they could be independent but still have someone nearby just in case."

Cheryl guessed that Lacey likely paid for the place as well, but she didn't ask. "Do you want me to wait in the car?"

"Oh no! Come on in with me. They'll love to meet you."

They walked through the main entrance and down a long corridor.

Lacey pointed toward a large common area that reminded Cheryl of a hunting lodge. Its hardwood floors, mahogany trim, and leather furniture were inviting, as was the fireplace and full bookcases. "This was the selling point for them. It doesn't feel institutional at all. Instead, it's rather like a very nice hotel that happens to offer medical care." She smiled at a group of elderly women seated at one of the tables playing cards. "This place has been the answer to a lot of prayer."

"I can see why." Cheryl made a mental note. She'd like to spend her own golden years in a place like this. "Can they have pets?"

Lacey laughed. "Don't tell me you're already planning for you and Beau to retire here."

"You caught me."

"Actually, yes. Small dogs and cats are allowed, but in the rooms only. And the residents have to be able to care for them. Nana and Papa brought their little Yorkie, Sassy. She's getting up there in years too." She paused outside of a door. The nameplate read Warren and Clara Landers. "Here we are." She knocked softly.

"Come in," a woman said.

Lacey opened the door and looked around the room. "Just making sure no one is in the room," she whispered to Cheryl. Once she saw that the coast was clear, she grinned widely. "Nana."

Clara Landers sat in a recliner, a white dog in her lap. Her face lit up at the sound of her granddaughter's voice. "Lacey!" She started to stand up, but Lacey rushed to her side. "Don't get up, Nana." She knelt down and hugged her tightly.

"What a nice surprise," Clara said. "Papa is asleep, but he'll be awake soon." She frowned. "You should've told me you were here."

Lacey laughed. "And ruin getting to see that look on your face? I'm so happy to see you." She leaned down and hugged her nana again. "I brought a friend with me." She motioned for Cheryl to come over to Clara's chair. "This is Cheryl Cooper. She's letting me stay with her in Sugarcreek for a few days."

Clara held out a wrinkled hand, and Cheryl took it.

"It's nice to meet you, Mrs. Landers. Lacey has been so excited about getting to see you."

Clara squeezed Cheryl's hand. "It's always nice to meet a friend of Lacey's. This must be the day for that."

Cheryl and Lacey exchanged a glance. "What do you mean, Nana?"

"A friend of yours was just here. In fact, I'm surprised you didn't run into him."

Lacey's face went pale. "Him? Do you know his name?"

Clara shook her head. "You know, it's funny. I'm not sure he ever told me."

"What did he say exactly?" Cheryl asked. She could see from the frozen expression on Lacey's face she was in no frame of mind to ask for details.

"Only that he admired Lacey very much. He said her work ethic was like no other. And he wondered if she'd been to see me lately." She scratched Sassy behind the ear. "I told him that she hadn't been here lately because of work, and he told me that was about to change." She reached up for Lacey, and the girl knelt down beside her grandmother. "And it looks like he was right because here you are."

"You say he just left?" Cheryl asked.

Clara nodded. "Just a few seconds before you came in."

They'd been talking and observing residents as they walked down the hall. Had they passed him? Cheryl glanced at Lacey. "You stay right here. I'm going to head out to see if I see anyone."

Lacey nodded.

Cheryl ran out the door and down the hallway, ignoring the strange looks. She reached the double doors and pushed them open.

Just as she came to a stop at the parking lot, she saw it.

The white car. Same as the one that had followed them to the Millers' the day the bus went missing. And presumably the same one that had followed Lacey home yesterday.

Who was it? And what did they want with Lacey?

Cheryl sank on to a bench and tried to catch her breath. One thing was clear: whoever was in the white car was getting bolder. They desperately needed to figure out who it was and what he wanted before he made another move.

And Cheryl was sure that he had something else planned. Visiting Lacey's grandmother was personal.

Cheryl added "keep Lacey safe" to her ever-growing list of things she needed to do.

Chapter Seventeen

Lacey was quiet on the car ride back to Sugarcreek. "Penny for your thoughts."

"I'm just wondering if I should be scared. Because I *am* scared. It's like one of those horror movies where you know the bad guy is about to jump out because of the music that's playing. But you jump anyway. I know this guy—or guys, because I am pretty sure there were two of them yesterday—is going to come around again. And what if he's not so nice the next time?" She sniffed. "What if Nana was in danger?"

The thought had crossed Cheryl's mind. "Maybe you should call and alert the administrator. I'm sure there's something they can do to help make your grandparents' room more secure, at least until we get to the bottom of things."

"Yeah, I'll do that. I know her, and she's a nice lady. She really cares about Nana and Papa, and I know she'll want to help keep them safe." She sighed. "I told Nana that the guy wasn't a friend. I think it worried her a lot—not for herself, but for me. But I promised her that we were being careful and keeping an eye on our surroundings. And she promised to keep the door closed and make people identify themselves before she tells them to come in. Not that that would *really* help if this guy is a real danger, but at least she knows to be extra cautious."

"That's good. And I think you should fill Roy in today when you're at lunch. He may want you to file some sort of report or something."

Lacey nodded. "I will. I hate to, but I will." She slouched in her seat. "I was so looking forward to just being a normal girl on a lunch date today. But now I have to bring my crazy life to the table instead."

"If it's any consolation, I saw the way Roy looked at you today." Cheryl smiled. "I don't think it matters to him one way or the other. Besides, he knows who you are in spite of how you're dressed. I imagine he has some idea what kind of challenges might occur in dating you. And yet he still asked you to lunch."

"Yeah, as Amish me. But it still remains to be seen whether he'll still want to see me after I'm out of a disguise and back to my everyday chaotic life."

Cheryl understood Lacey's worry, but from the look on Roy's face this morning when he'd been talking to Lacey, she was pretty sure the girl had nothing to worry about.

She parked near the Swiss Miss, and they got out of the car.

"Thank you for taking me to see them. I really appreciate it. Papa finally woke up and was so happy to see me. They asked me to come back tomorrow." She smiled. "I think I'll ask Roy if he'll give me a ride—provided today goes okay."

Cheryl nodded. "Sounds good. If you end up needing a ride from me though, I'll be glad to. Or you can borrow my car."

She hardly ever loaned her vehicle to anyone, but she felt like the circumstance demanded it.

"Thanks."

They greeted Esther and Lydia at the counter. Both girls were waiting on customers.

Naomi still sat at the desk in the storeroom. She looked up when they came in.

"Any progress?" Cheryl asked.

Naomi looked thoughtful. "Maybe. I had an idea that might be worth looking into."

"Well don't leave us hanging!" Lacey plopped down next to her. "What is it?"

"What would motivation be for someone to make your tour bus disappear?" Naomi asked.

Cheryl shrugged. "I don't know. I guess if someone wanted to get revenge on me for something. Or on your family. Or on someone onboard." She widened her eyes and stared at Naomi. "You're a genius."

"I'm lost." Lacey patted the desk as if bringing a meeting to attention.

"I don't know about the passengers on the tour bus, but I do know someone who was pretty upset with me. Richard Wellaby." Cheryl frowned. "Mean Richard."

"That guy the people at the bookstore were telling us about? You really think he could've had something to do with it?"

"It makes sense. He was furious. And the last thing he said to me was that I hadn't heard the last of him."

Naomi nodded. "I think it is worth looking into."

Cheryl agreed. "We'll swing by his place today. He doesn't live too far from Mickey." She motioned to the front of the store. "I'm going to go relieve Esther and Lydia for a little while so they can have a lunch break. Once they get back, I'll be ready to go."

Cheryl helped a couple of customers choose their souvenirs and then rang up their purchases. The past two days had been so hectic, she'd forgotten how soothing it could be to get back to a normal routine. She could almost forget about the situation, except that Lacey hovered nearby, pausing every now and then to ask about some of the merchandise.

Roy walked into the Swiss Miss, a frown on his handsome face.

"Is everything okay?" Cheryl asked. She'd been hoping he'd come back with good news, but from the looks of him it was the opposite.

"No fingerprints could be lifted. They tried." He shrugged. "Nothing more they could do."

"I'm sorry," Lacey said. "But here's some good news. Cheryl and Naomi are going to go hunt for Mickey. They think if they find him, they can find the bus." She smiled. "And they're also going to stop and talk to that mean Richard guy who was all bent out of shape that the tour was going on."

Cheryl groaned inwardly. She'd planned to keep their sleuthing a secret until they were done. It was her experience that it generally went more smoothly that way.

Roy narrowed his eyes. "I know that this morning I told you to go to a couple of stores nearby and see if they may have seen someone put this box on your stoop. And that was fine. But going after people who could be involved with the bus disappearing is another story."

"Wait. You think Mickey could be involved?" Cheryl asked. "Or Richard?"

"I think that everyone is a suspect until I am sure they aren't. Your driver hasn't been seen or heard from since Thursday." He frowned. "And this is the first I've heard of Richard."

"Does that mean you've checked on Mickey?" Now Cheryl was intrigued. Did Roy know more about the bus than he was letting on?

"It means that I am following all leads. And until we know exactly what we're dealing with, I hope you and Naomi will be careful." He raked a hand through his hair. "I guess this is the kind of stuff the chief was referring to?"

Cheryl nodded. "I don't see anything wrong with us driving out to Mickey's house just to check if he's back. Or if we see anything unusual. He's our friend." Well, he was Naomi's friend. Cheryl barely knew the guy, and for all she knew, maybe he *was* some kind of crazy bus-driving kidnapper. "And Richard was so bent out of shape over the tour. I don't think it would hurt to just stop by and try to smooth things over. If he had anything to do with the disappearance, I think we'll be able to tell. He doesn't exactly have a poker face." He mostly just had an angry face, but that was another story.

"Just promise that you'll be careful," Roy said. "If you see anything out of the ordinary at all, call me. Or call Chief Twitchell.

Please don't put yourself in any kind of danger. We already have enough to deal with."

Cheryl nodded. "I promise, we won't." She told Lacey and Roy to have a good time and watched as they left the store, totally caught up in their conversation. As much as she'd love to have her own lunch date, she was happy for Lacey. In spite of their differences, they really seemed to mesh well together. Hopefully that would remain true even after Lacey had dropped her Amish persona and was back to being a pop star/actress.

Lydia and Esther walked up to the counter chattering about the things teenage girls chatter about. From what she could gather, Lydia had a boyfriend and Esther had her eye on someone. But Cheryl didn't want to pry.

"Will you girls be okay minding the store for a little while on your own this afternoon?"

"Ja." Esther nodded. "We'll be fine."

Cheryl smiled. "Thanks." She stepped to the back room. "Are you ready?"

Naomi stood. "I am. I hope this will give us some answers. Finally."

"Have you been to Mickey's house before?" Cheryl asked once she and Naomi left the store.

"Last year when his wife passed away. I took him a few casseroles and some bread and jam." She shook her head. "It was really a difficult time for him. They were a great couple. Very much in love. When they first moved to Sugarcreek, he worked on our farm for a time. That's how we know him."

"Do you think he is involved?"

Naomi shook her head. "Mickey does not have a mean bone in his body. If he is still driving that bus, then there is a reason."

"Meaning he is being forced?"

Naomi shrugged. "I do not believe he would do anything that could harm the tour group."

Maybe not, but if they could find out more about him, maybe they could get some kind of clue as to where the group might be. "How about Richard?"

"He is another case," Naomi admitted. "I have watched him have disagreements with so many people. I wish I could say that he is not capable of such a thing, but I think he might be."

"Let's stop by his place first." Cheryl had looked up his address on her phone before they left the store. He lived a few blocks over from Mickey.

Cheryl pulled into the driveway next to a Ford pickup truck. "Guess he's home."

"You sound apprehensive."

Cheryl laughed. "I guess I am. More than anything I just wish I could avoid the confrontation I know will be waiting."

"I do not blame you. He has not been that pleasant to deal with, especially in recent years." Naomi cleared her throat. "But there was a time, years ago, when he was not so bad."

"Really?" She hadn't heard anything but bad where Richard was concerned.

Naomi nodded. "It has been my experience that people react to bad things in their lives one of two ways. Either they take them in stride and allow them to help shape and mold them into stronger people or they dwell on the negative until it eats them up. I think you can guess which way Richard went."

"What happened to him?"

"It was actually Mitzi who told me the story. She and Richard have known one another since they were young. I always wondered if that is why he was particularly nasty to her—because she knew him well and knew his secrets."

Secrets? Cheryl was curious now. "What could possibly justify his behavior?"

"I do not mean to offer an excuse for him. He should not let the past cloud his future. But he does. He clings to the bitterness of what might have been instead of looking toward what could be." Naomi smiled. "When Richard was a young man, he fell in love with a girl from right here in Sugarcreek. Her name was Lottie Yoder." She paused and glanced at Cheryl.

"She was Amish?" Cheryl asked.

Naomi nodded. "They met because she worked at Richard's mother's bakery in town. According to Mitzi, he was completely smitten. For a time, he wanted to become Amish, and Mitzi thinks he would have if it would have helped his case."

"But Lottie wasn't interested?"

Naomi sighed. "I do not believe that was the case. It seems that Lottie shared his feelings, but she did not believe it could ever work out. She saw them as being from two different worlds and was certain that those differences would bring them too much strife."

Cheryl frowned. "That's a sad story."

Naomi nodded. "Lottie joined the church the year she turned eighteen. Soon after that, she and Noah Byler were published to be married. When Richard heard the news, he went to her home and begged her to tell him how she felt about him and call off her wedding. But Lottie would have nothing to do with him. According to Mitzi, that was the last time she ever remembers Richard being nice to anyone. From that point forward, he let his bitterness swallow him."

"It seems as if he would've moved away from here, what with the bad memories and all." Cheryl had to admit, it was a sad story. But she agreed with Naomi. He would've been better off to leave the past and seek happiness without Lottie.

"Lottie and Noah are the ones who moved. They went to Indiana to help one of Noah's relatives, and they ended up settling there. I guess Richard figured he may as well stay in the only place he'd ever called home."

A loud rap on Cheryl's window startled both women.

Richard snarled at them through the car window. "What do you want?"

Cheryl took a breath. "I'm going to get out and talk to him. If things get too ugly, honk the horn or something."

Naomi chuckled. "I will."

Cheryl opened the door and stood face-to-face with Richard. "Sorry to bother you, Mr. Wellaby," she started.

"Well then don't." He cut her off. "Whatever you're sellin' I don't need."

She sighed. He sure didn't make things easy. "I'm not actually selling anything. I just came to ask you a couple of questions."

"Like what?" he sneered.

Cheryl took a deep breath. She'd debated whether to come clean to him just to see if she could pick up on guilt. She decided to bite the bullet and go for it. "The Live Like the Amish Tour never made it to its destination."

Richard blinked, wide-eyed. "What do you mean?"

"The bus and everyone onboard has disappeared. I was hoping you might know something about it."

He was silent for a long moment. "Mickey too?"

Of course he'd know Mickey. He probably had him drive for some of his own tours. "Yes."

Richard furrowed his brow. "I don't know nothin' about it. I'm sure you'll be blamin' me all over town for the disappearance."

She shook her head. "No. I won't. I just wanted to be sure you didn't know anything about it. That's all." She wanted to say something more. Offer him some kind of peace offering. She opened the car door. "Thanks for your time." She started to get in then stood back up. "And Richard, I don't know if you already have a church home, but if not, you're welcome to visit Silo Church. We'd love to have you." She closed the door before he could respond, but not before she saw his shocked expression.

"What did you do to leave him speechless?" Naomi asked as they pulled out of his driveway.

"Invited him to church. I figure since he's alienated pretty much the whole town, not many people have been knocking down his door to invite him. So I figured I'd do it. He doesn't care for me anyway." She grinned.

Naomi chuckled. "I will add him to my prayer list. Perhaps he will come to understand that so long as he has breath, it is not too late to change his ways."

Cheryl nodded. "Those are words to live by."

Chapter Eighteen

Mickey Simmons's red brick home was small but well kept. The yard and carport were tidy, and the shutters and trim were recently painted. Mickey's old pickup sat in the carport, but there was no sign of the bus.

"Does he normally park the bus here?" Cheryl asked.

Naomi nodded. "Ja."

As expected, the bus was nowhere to be seen.

They got out of the vehicle and walked up the sidewalk to his door. Cheryl knocked then rang the doorbell.

They stood for a few minutes and waited.

"Just as we thought. He's gone." Cheryl stood on her tiptoes and peeked in the mailbox next to the door.

"Cheryl!" Naomi said.

She laughed. "Just peeking. I wasn't going to go through it or anything. But it definitely looks like he hasn't been here since he left on Thursday morning."

Naomi nodded. "He was supposed to return back here each evening. There is something wrong. I do not think he would just leave without making arrangements for his mail. Do you?"

"Who knows?" Cheryl walked to the carport and peered inside his old truck. She checked the driver's side door. It opened. "It's unlocked. I'm just going to take a peek to see if there is anything that might give us a clue."

Naomi opened the passenger door. "I suppose this is okay. We are only trying to help Mickey." She lifted a stack of papers from the seat and shuffled through them.

"I don't know that there's anything in here that's helpful. I mostly see candy wrappers and gas station receipts," Cheryl said after a moment. "How about you?"

Naomi held up a small piece of folded notebook paper. "Look at this." She unfolded the paper. Scrawled in ink were the words: *Your debt is forgiven if you do as we ask. $15,000 becomes $0.* "Do you think this could have anything to do with the missing bus?"

Cheryl shrugged. "Who knows? That's a lot of money though."

They agreed that the note was best left where they found it. As they headed back to Cheryl's car, a woman across the street called out to them.

Cheryl and Naomi walked across the street to where the woman stood in her driveway. She was plump and wore a flowered house dress that Cheryl's momma would call a muumuu.

"I'm Cheryl, and this is Naomi." Cheryl flashed a smile.

"You lookin' for Mick?" she asked, eyeing them suspiciously.

Cheryl nodded. "We are. We're friends of his, and he's been running a tour for me. Do you know where he is?"

"My name is Barbara, and I sure don't." She shook her head. "He hasn't been around in a couple of days. It's odd. Last time I talked to him, he said he'd be home nights. I've got a key to the house, and I go in and feed his cat when he's out with a tour group." Her voice was raspy like a chain smoker's. "He's been so out of sorts since Wanda died. I try to look in on him when I can, but I've never known him to just not come home when he's s'posed to. Poor Tabby."

They looked at her with matching blank expressions.

"The cat. Tabby Cat. Not the most original name in the world, but that's what it is." She smiled. "Anyway, I've been going over twice a day since he's been gone just so she won't get lonely."

"That's very kind of you. I'm sure he'll really appreciate that when he gets back," Cheryl said. "Um, did you notice anything odd about his house?"

The woman shook her head. "Don't guess so. There's a big stack of bills on the table that need stamps. Guess he's got a lot of stuff to pay off." She shrugged. "None of my business though."

Cheryl handed her a card from the Swiss Miss. "If you hear from Mickey, will you let me know? I need to talk to him about a tour."

She nodded. "I sure will."

They thanked her for helping Mickey out and headed back to the car.

"Do you think that big stack of bills ready to mail has anything to do with the note you found?"

"I have no idea," Naomi said. "I'm sure there are a lot of medical bills left from Wanda's illness. She was sick for a very long time. I can see that someone erasing a fifteen thousand dollar debt could be helpful to him." She looked over at Cheryl. "But that doesn't mean he harmed a bus full of people."

Maybe not. But it did mean something. Cheryl just had to find out what and maybe she could get to the bottom of things once and for all.

When Cheryl and Naomi arrived back at the Swiss Miss, a surprise was waiting for them in the form of Chief Twitchell. He and Lacey stood at the counter talking, and they looked up when Cheryl and Naomi walked in the store.

"Good afternoon, ladies." Twitchell nodded at them then eyed Cheryl. "I understand you have a little somethin' you need to report."

Her face flamed. "About that. I'm so sorry. I thought the bus disappearance was being handled by the FBI, but come to find out, they weren't real agents."

Twitchell nodded. "Mr. Neal apprised me of the situation. I'm gonna have some questions for you, I'm sure, but I just wanted to stop in and make sure you'd let me know if anything else happens."

"I promise, I will." Cheryl wondered if she could be considered at fault for not reporting the disappearance, even though she had been duped by Riggins and McGraw. "I don't know what all Roy has told you, but I've received two phone calls that let me know the tour group was safe. After a little digging, I found out the calls came from the phone shed that belongs to the Troyer family. And then someone dropped off Lacey's bag this morning." She shrugged. "But I guess you already know about that."

"Mr. Neal used our resources to test for fingerprints. As for the calls, he told me that too. It tells me that your whistle-blower is someone familiar with the town. Probably someone you know. It appears to me that the reason for contactin' you is because he or she is worried about your involvement in the tour. They want you to know the people are okay."

Cheryl had already come to the same conclusion. "Yes. I think so too."

"Do you have any idea why the bus and the people on it may have gone missing?"

"No. I thought maybe it had something to do with Lacey, but since she is obviously not on the tour now, it seems unlikely to me that it would be about her. And I don't think it has to do with Roy's grandma either, since Riggins and McGraw are the ones after her and they didn't get here until after the bus was already gone." She sighed. "I have no ideas."

Twitchell eyed her for a long moment as if to size up if she were telling the truth. He finally seemed satisfied that she was. "Very well. If you think of anything, don't hesitate to call me. And if you get another one of those calls, let me know." He sighed. "We don't know what we're dealing with here, Cheryl. Don't go chasin' after that bus alone."

She didn't have any plans to chase after it alone. She'd have Naomi or Lacey with her, of course. But telling that to Twitchell wasn't a good idea. "I don't plan to put myself in harm's way." Complete and utter truth.

"Very good." He nodded his good-bye. "I'll be in touch."

Once he was gone, she pulled Lacey aside. "How did it go today?"

She giggled. "We had a great time."

Cheryl was much less interested in how the love connection was going than she was in whether Roy had made any headway at all. "Did you find anything new?"

"Well, first I told Roy all about those two men in the white car. He just thinks we should keep an eye out. And he doesn't want me to go anywhere alone." She smiled broadly. "He's going to take me to Dover tomorrow, so you're off the hook."

Cheryl was glad Lacey had filled Roy in on the two mystery men. "Anything else? Especially pertaining to the bus?"

"Kind of," Lacey said. "We talked to a lady at the restaurant where we ate lunch. I described Riggins and McGraw, and she said they'd been in there asking about the bus driver guy. But she didn't know him so she had nothing to tell them. Roy is contacting some of the hotels nearby to see if they are staying at any of them."

Cheryl sighed.

"What's wrong?" Naomi asked. She'd been listening to their exchange.

"It keeps occurring to me that finding Riggins and McGraw—and even finding out what they want with Roy's grandma—doesn't help us find the bus. You know? I don't think one will lead to the other."

"That may be so, but if we can eliminate the threat that those two men pose, Roy's grandmother will be safer once we do find the group." She put a reassuring hand on Cheryl's arm. "And we will find them."

"I sure hope you're right."

Time was running out. Cheryl couldn't help but think of the activities they'd planned for the group today. It was a beautiful

Saturday—cold, but sunny. January days got a bad reputation for being gray and gloomy, but this one had bright blue skies and fluffy white clouds. It would've been the perfect day for the tour group to be at the Millers' farm, helping to care for their many animals and touring the property.

But what was the group doing instead?

Cheryl said a silent prayer that wherever they were, they were each somehow happy, safe, and enjoying the day.

Chapter Nineteen

Just before the Swiss Miss closed for the day, Roy rushed inside. "It's Grandma!" he exclaimed, waving his cell phone in the air. "She called and left me a voice mail." He was out of breath by the time he reached the counter.

Cheryl widened her eyes. "What did she say?" Her heart beat a little faster. Would this be the break they were hoping for?

"You won't believe this." He set the phone on the counter and hit Play.

"Hi, Roy. It's Grandma." Her voice was much more chipper than it had been the day she ran into the Swiss Miss and joined the tour. "I've had a hard time getting a signal. I just wanted you to know that I'm having a wonderful time on the tour. The Millers are so sweet and, oh, the food is just delicious! I'll try to call again soon. I love you, dear."

Naomi gasped. "The Millers? How can that be?"

"It makes no sense." Cheryl picked up the phone and stared at the screen as if it would give her the answers to all of their questions. "Have you been able to get in touch with her since she left the message?"

"No. I tried to call her back as soon as I heard it, but it went to her voice mail."

"She sounded happy though," Lacey observed. "She wasn't scared or anything, so I guess she really believes she is with the Millers."

"But she is not." Naomi shook her head. "I am more confused now than ever."

Roy put his phone back in his pocket. "Are there any other Millers around the area?"

"Maybe not within a few miles, but Miller is a common name in the area. I'd guess there are a lot of families with that last name near here—Charm, Dover, Berlin, and even Millersburg are nearby." Cheryl shrugged. "I have no idea how we'd go about tracking down all the Millers."

Roy sighed. "I was hoping you'd have some suggestions. I'm at a loss at this point."

She knew what he meant. It was beginning to seem like the group would be gone forever. On Monday, the bus was supposed to head back to the airport. If all those people didn't show up for flights, the whole country would end up finding out about the missing bus. Sugarcreek would be on the map for something besides cheese and fry pies. "We went to Mickey's today."

Roy furrowed his brow. "I was hoping you were leaving the investigating to the professionals."

Sometimes amateurs could find out more than professionals for the simple fact that they didn't carry the stigma of police. At least that had been Cheryl's experience. But she didn't point it out to him. "We weren't in danger or anything. But we did find a couple of interesting things." She filled him in on the note from the truck and their encounter with Barbara. "I think Mickey is somehow involved."

"Oh, I do not think so," Naomi said. "He is a good man who has had a tough time since Wanda passed away. I do not think he would bring harm to anyone."

"Grandma didn't sound like she was unhappy though. She sounded normal."

"Maybe someone was forcing her to do that?" Lacey piped up. "In my TV movie, *Call or I'll Shoot*, I had to make a call while there was a gun to my head and I had to say that everything was fine."

Roy grimaced.

Cheryl made a mental note to have a Netflix marathon of Lacey Landers movies when this ordeal was all said and done. She wasn't sure they were all meant to be comedies, but based on the titles she'd heard so far, she was guessing they were full of unintentional humor.

"Oh, but I'm sure that's not what is going on here." Lacey's voice was so cheery it reminded Cheryl of a high school cheerleader. "I'm sure your grandma is just fine."

Eager to move on, Cheryl turned her attention to Esther. The girl was stocking a shelf with the homemade candles Cheryl liked so much. "How were things here while we were gone?"

Esther stopped and smiled, looking very much like a younger version of Naomi. "Not bad. We only had a few customers. You missed another one of Ben and Rueben's rousing games of checkers."

"I hate that I missed them." And it was true. Although some people counted down the hours till their work day was over, Cheryl genuinely enjoyed the time she spent working at the Swiss Miss. She enjoyed the people of Sugarcreek who stopped by, like the Vogel brothers. She was fortunate to have the perspective of someone who'd been in a career not suited for her. Now that she was managing the Swiss Miss, she felt like she was finally doing something she was good at and something she was passionate about. It was a good feeling.

"Lydia already left, but she wanted me to tell you something," Esther said. "Her brother, Thomas, came by earlier. He said that this morning there had been someone parked by the road and he could see that they were headed to the phone shed. But when the guy saw him, he ran and got back in his truck."

So maybe the mysterious caller had planned to give Cheryl another message this morning. "Did Thomas get a look at the man?"

Esther shook her head. "He said he was all bundled up for the cold weather. Even his face was covered up. He didn't recognize the truck either. It was old and green. That's all he knew."

Roy smiled at her. "Thank you for the information. I'll contact Chief Twitchell and see if he can send someone out to see if there might be any fingerprints in the shed. Although considering the cold, it's likely the guy has worn gloves each time."

"You're probably right," Cheryl agreed.

Esther and Naomi left, followed closely by Lacey and Roy. "I'll see you at Aunt Mitzi's cottage in a bit," she said.

Lacey nodded. "Okay."

The store was quiet. Esther had hung the Closed sign as she walked out the door.

What a day.

Just before they left, Naomi had invited them all over to their farm for dinner. Cheryl had to admit she was glad—not just because she enjoyed their company, but because she had an empty cupboard at home. She'd expected to be with the tour group for the majority of the weekend and hadn't planned on having to house and feed a houseguest.

The bell above the door jingled, and Kathy walked in. "I know you're closed, so I won't keep you long."

Cheryl laughed. "Don't be silly."

"First I wanted to check in to see if you had any news on your bus."

Cheryl filled her in on all the events since they'd last spoken. "It seems like we take one step forward and three back."

"Maybe it will all add up soon. I have faith that you'll put the whole puzzle together."

Cheryl groaned. "I'm glad you think so. Because I'm beginning to wonder if any of it will ever make sense." She took off her Swiss Miss apron and stowed it under the counter. "How about you? Any new developments with Michael Rogers?"

"Actually...yes." Kathy ran her fingers through her hair. "I saw him today at Wallhouse Coffee. He was with another guy. They appeared to be having a business meeting of some sort. Both had iPads, and the other guy had a phone permanently attached to his ear."

"Any idea who the other man is?"

"Never seen him before. But they had that same look—fit and way too tan to be from around here."

Cheryl laughed. "I noticed that about Michael when I saw him at your café. I thought he seemed like he belonged on a surfboard or something."

"Exactly."

"Did he ever tell Heather where he was from?"

Kathy shook her head. "Kind of. He claims to have had homes in lots of places. North Carolina, Florida, California." She shrugged. "Who knows the truth with this guy?"

"Heather told me they were going out again tonight to do a little sightseeing."

Kathy nodded. "I'm hopeful that she'll put an end to the whole thing tonight, and then I can stop worrying about it. I think she's beginning to wonder if he is on the up-and-up."

"At least she figured it out for herself. That's much better than her buying every line and then being devastated."

"My thoughts exactly." Kathy looked at her watch. "I'd better get going. Please keep me posted about the bus."

Cheryl nodded. "I sure will." She locked the store behind her and headed home.

Chapter Twenty

"Are you sure Naomi doesn't mind letting us see their farm and eat dinner with her family?" Lacey asked.

"They were prepared to host a fairly large group this weekend, so I don't think we'll be imposing at all." Cheryl was secretly delighted at the chance to spend a little extra time around Levi. "I'm just sad it's dark and you won't get to see much of the place. When there are no streetlights to light the way, it is a different kind of darkness."

"I'll bet." Lacey sank on to the couch. "Roy is going to meet us there. I think he had some work to do from the hotel this afternoon. He's trying to see if his grandma's cell phone can be pinged to find a location. I hope it can. Day after tomorrow will be here before we know, and it'll be time for those people to return home." She removed her prayer kapp and let her hair down. "Oh, that hurts," she said, massaging her scalp. "My hair is so thick, it kind of gives me a headache to keep it up like this all the time." A mischievous smile spread across her face. "Maybe tonight I could be an Amish girl in 'roomspringer' or however you say it. And wear regular clothes?"

Cheryl laughed. "Rumspringa. And I guess that's up to you."

Lacey flung herself over on the couch and placed her hand to her forehead. "I think I shouldn't do it. It's tempting though. Roy hasn't seen me in my real clothes before."

"I would be tempted too. Any word from Blake lately? Has the guy reached out to you or to him after visiting your nana?"

"No." Lacey held up her phone. "But Blake texted me earlier and said he'd had a call from a reporter who claimed to have photos of me in Sugarcreek. I guess one is going to be in *US Weekly* tomorrow as confirmation that I'm here. If that happens, we may have some trouble." She sighed. "So I guess tonight I'll just try to blend in with the Miller family as best as I can." She grinned. "I stopped by that other thrift store earlier though—you know, the one that's across from the Honey Bee Café? I bought another Amish dress, and this one is a pretty light blue color. I think I'll wear it tonight." She jumped up and headed to the guest room, Beau at her feet.

Cheryl looked in her own closet. It was sweet to watch Lacey want to look pretty for Roy, even though she was in disguise. She turned her attention to her own wardrobe. Levi had commented once about her green eyes, so she decided to wear a green sweater that exactly matched them. She quickly paired the sweater with dark jeans and threw on a multicolored scarf to complete the look. Not bad. She raked her hand through her spiky red hair and wondered for the millionth time whether she should grow it out.

Images of herself with big hair flashed through her mind. Nope. Her wild hair was best tamed by a short cut.

As they pulled out of the driveway, Lacey turned off the radio. "Is there anything I should know? I mean, I went with you to that house the other day to ask about the bus, but that was the first time I have ever been in an Amish home. I don't want to mess up and say the wrong thing."

Cheryl completely understood the girl's angst. "They aren't really much different from the rest of us. Just remember that. At their core, they are just people. They love to laugh and eat and spend time with the ones they love. Just like we do."

"Maybe I am overthinking it, huh?" Lacey asked.

"At Naomi's and Seth's, the kitchen is the heart of their home. Whenever I've visited them, we've almost always ended up there. Naomi does a lot of baking, and the family is very close-knit. So you can often find one or more of them helping in the kitchen or just in there talking to her."

"Okay. I get it. That was the way things were at Nana's. She was always cooking something, and usually you could find one of her kids or grandkids in the kitchen with her."

Each time Lacey mentioned her nana's house, her voice filled with nostalgia and longing. Cheryl wished she could figure out how to encourage the girl to spend some time with her family for a visit. It was obvious how dear her grandparents were to her, and Cheryl knew they wouldn't be around forever. But she bit her tongue. Perhaps she didn't know Lacey well enough to give her such personal advice. "That sounds nice."

"It was. I guess I had a pretty idyllic childhood and didn't even realize it at the time."

Cheryl nodded. "I think most of us are that way. Kind of that whole 'you don't know what you've got till it's gone' thing." She glanced over at Lacey and realized she hadn't heard much about her lunch date with Roy. "So I'm glad you and Roy had fun today. Do you plan to see him after you go back home?"

"I hope so. But I'm sort of putting that ball in his court. I mean, I'm not going to chase after him or anything. He's really different than any guy I've gone out with since I've been a grown-up." She laughed. "Sounds weird, I know, but I left home right after high school graduation. Pretty much all the relationships I've had as an adult have been with people in the entertainment industry. Sometimes it gets tough to know the real from the fake. But Roy... He's not pretending to be anything but who he is. I like that. I also like that I can tell he's interested in me, and I don't think that has anything to do with the fact that my face has been on the cover of *People* more times than I can count. You know?"

He did seem like a genuine kind of guy. "That's nice. I hope you do keep in touch with him. I'm sure he'll be a breath of fresh air for you."

Cheryl turned from the main road on to the road that led to the Millers' house. "I wish we'd been able to come out here today during the day. You really could've seen the property then." She slowed down so she could point out the landmarks to Lacey. "That's where they have a corn maze during the fall. It's very popular. They have a petting zoo as well. Their farm is open to the public, and people love the various animals."

"Oh, I've never driven through a covered bridge before," Lacey exclaimed as they crossed the water. "It's so cool."

"You know, the Amish call those kissing bridges," Cheryl said.

"What? Do tell."

Cheryl laughed. "When an Amish couple is courting and they drive their buggy through a kissing bridge, they just might go a little slower than need be so they can steal a kiss without anyone seeing."

"That's so romantic. Don't you just love it?" Lacey asked. "How cool would it be to go on a date in a horse and buggy and have the guy drive you through a covered bridge so he could steal a kiss?"

Cheryl thought so too. In fact, she hated to admit it, but she'd actually thought a little about whom she might like to travel through a covered bridge with. And every time she pictured it, it was the same person.

Levi Miller.

She'd ridden with him in his buggy a couple of times, but they were just friends. They'd certainly never paused to take advantage of a kissing bridge. Cheryl pushed that thought from her head and parked her Ford Focus next to a buggy near the Millers' house. The white farmhouse had a wraparound porch that Cheryl adored. The house always seemed so homey despite its large size.

"It's so pretty," Lacey said. "And believe me, I know real estate. I just bought a place."

Cheryl didn't want to admit she'd done a little Google stalking and already knew about the recent purchase. "That's great."

Headlights appeared at the end of the bridge, then Roy's SUV emerged. "Looks like we just barely beat him," Lacey said. She smoothed her dress and grinned.

Roy pulled in beside them and got out of the car. "Hello, ladies." It was easy to see why Lacey was attracted to him. He reminded her of a younger version of George Clooney. Not to mention that he was a genuinely nice guy.

"We are so glad all of you could come for dinner," Levi said, stepping out on to the porch. "Maam has been cooking up a storm, and it smells delicious."

Cheryl's heart skipped a beat at the sight of him. She was going to have to get this crush she had under control. Although she wasn't sure it was just a crush. Did thirty-year-old women really have crushes? It was easy to tell herself and others, like Lacey, that she and Levi were only friends, but then she got around him and her heart beat faster and she heard herself giggling like a school girl. She vowed to put off the analysis of their relationship for another day—or ten—and just enjoy tonight. "Hi, Levi." She smiled.

He returned her smile. "How are you? Are you still chastising yourself over the missing bus?"

She nodded. "Kind of. I sure hoped we'd have them located by now." She sighed. "At least the authorities are involved now, so surely they'll turn up soon."

"We are all praying that will be the case." He ushered them into the living room.

The fireplace burned, filling the large room with warmth. "That feels so good," Cheryl said. "There's nothing better than wood heat."

"Unless your job is to split the logs and bring them inside," Levi teased.

She laughed. "True."

The modestly decorated room was inviting, with gleaming hardwood floors and a beautiful mahogany china cabinet.

Cheryl introduced Lacey and Roy to the Miller family. "You've met Naomi and Esther already. This is Naomi's husband, Seth."

Seth stepped forward and offered a hand. "Welcome."

"And this is Levi."

Lacey grinned. "We met the other day."

Cheryl felt Lacey's eyes on her but refused to meet them. "And Caleb." She was struck again by how much alike Levi and Caleb looked. They were both blond like their biological mother had been, a sharp contrast to Naomi's biological children who were all dark haired like she was.

"You know Esther," she said.

Esther smiled. "Nice to see you again."

"Elizabeth is the older sister, but if you saw them from a distance, you'd have a hard time telling them apart."

Elizabeth laughed. "Ja. We get mistaken for twins sometimes even."

"Eli will not be joining us. He is helping out at a friend's farm over in Millersburg. He will be back tomorrow evening though," Seth explained.

"The food is ready," Naomi said, gesturing toward the kitchen.

They followed her inside, and Cheryl remembered what she'd told Lacey about the Millers' home. The kitchen was definitely the heart of the house. A wooden table sat in the middle of the room, large enough to accommodate the entire family and then some. It was already set for dinner.

Roy eyed the food that sat on a long wooden sideboard along the wall. "Wow. That's quite a spread." He rubbed his hands together. "I can't remember the last time I had a home-cooked meal."

"Please, be seated." Seth motioned toward the table.

Cheryl caught Lacey staring at the gas-powered lantern that hung above the table. She should've taken time to explain a few of the differences that could be found in an Amish home, like gas-powered lighting, gas-range stoves, and the propane-fueled refrigerator. She made a mental note to tell her about it when they got back to the cottage. One thing was certain—by the time Lacey arrived at the movie set, she should be very comfortable in an Amish setting.

Now if they could just get through dinner without Lacey's normal barrage of questions, everything would be fine.

"Do y'all only drink water?" Lacey whispered loudly to Esther. "Or are you allowed to drink Cokes too?"

Esther and Elizabeth giggled.

So much for the hope of no questions.

Chapter Twenty-One

After a delicious dinner that included pot roast, mashed potatoes, and homemade bread, Levi led Cheryl, Lacey, and Roy outside. "I know it is dark, but we have a gas lantern in the barn." They walked past the pasture and two horses whinnied. "Samson wants a little attention."

Cheryl rubbed the big horse's muzzle. "He's so beautiful." She hadn't grown up around horses, but now that she was in Sugarcreek, she saw them on a daily basis. There was something so majestic about the big creatures.

"I had to ride a horse once for my music video, *Not My First Rodeo*," Lacey said. "Bless his heart, we had to do the same take over and over again. Do you know how hard it is to sing and hold a guitar while riding a horse on the beach? Those things don't all go together."

Roy laughed. "You sure have had some interesting experiences."

"Yeah, but I think being here in Sugarcreek is my favorite one." Lacey only had eyes for Roy.

Cheryl fell into step alongside Levi. She was beginning to feel like she was a third wheel on someone else's date. Lacey and Roy trailed behind, lost in their own conversation. "I'm glad we got to come over tonight. Dinner was delicious."

He glanced over at her. "Me too. I have been worried about you since the bus disappeared. It is not your fault, you know."

She nodded. "I didn't physically take them somewhere, but I still feel partially responsible. And Chief Twitchell got the list of emergency contacts from me this morning. I don't know if he has already called them or not. But he has them now. I hate for their families to worry." She furrowed her brow. "What if some of them are like Roy's grandma? And they've called home to say they are having a good time? None of it makes any sense."

They reached the barn, and Levi opened the door. "These are the petting zoo animals," he explained to Roy and Lacey. "Feel free to look around. They are used to people and are very tame." He pointed to a large container. "And if you want them to love you, get some food in your hand to offer them." Once Roy and Lacey were making the rounds in the barn, Levi turned his attention back to her. "I agree. None of it makes sense now. But things have a way of working out."

"I guess. At least I no longer feel as if they may be in danger. Now I'm just curious. Who would go to the trouble to do something like this? And more importantly, why?"

"I am having a hard time believing the bus driver was not involved, even though Maam defends him." Levi smiled. "She only wants to see the best in people."

"I know. I wish I could be more like that. But Mickey has disappeared, just like the bus." She shrugged. "If he wasn't somehow involved, then why haven't we heard from him?"

"Maybe you have..." Levi trailed off.

"I wondered about that too. But why not just come out and tell us how to find the group? Why call in a way that I can't get back in touch with him?"

Levi smiled. "I have no answers. Only guesses. But I have known Mickey for a while now. I tend to agree with Naomi that he is not a bad guy. Maybe he is just trying to let you know the group is safe."

"Which is sweet. But what I want to know is *where* are they safe?"

"Always full of questions. Maybe you missed your calling." Levi raised an eyebrow. "Perhaps you should have been a detective instead of a shopkeeper."

She laughed. "I don't think so." She looked up at him. "What about you? If you hadn't been born here, on a farm, what would you have wanted to be?"

His blue eyes grew thoughtful. "I enjoy making those Bible covers that you sell in the store." When Cheryl had first moved to town, she'd seen some of his work and encouraged him to offer his products at the Swiss Miss. It had taken some convincing, but the leather Bible covers were now a popular item. "I think I would probably do something along those lines. Maybe a leather goods store." He grinned. "But for now I get to do both—help my family with their farm and all that's involved, and also work on the Bible covers for you."

"Well I don't think I would've ever chosen to be a detective." She glanced over and watched as Lacey and Roy discussed something intently. That seemed to be going well. "I consider it such a blessing that I left the banking world. I know I wouldn't want to go back. Actually I'm happy at the Swiss Miss. It's the kind of job that not only fulfills me, it also seems to give me a connection to the town. I like that."

"You really like it in Sugarcreek, don't you?" he asked softly.

She nodded. "I do. There have been times over the months that I've questioned whether this is my path. But the longer I'm here, the more convinced I am that it is."

"Good." His eyes bored into hers. "Because I do not want you to go anywhere."

She'd always hated the expression about butterflies in the stomach, but she knew if she had to describe the moment later, that's the only way she could explain it. That and the fact that she felt warm with happiness despite the winter chill outside.

Once they'd returned to the cottage, Cheryl turned on her laptop. She checked her e-mail, and one jumped out at her. Aunt Mitzi.

She eagerly opened it and began to read.

My dearest Cheryl,

    I hope this finds you well. I admit, I was a bit concerned with your last message. A missing bus! I'm praying that those people are found and there is a reasonable explanation. Dear girl, I hope you don't blame yourself. I know you and Levi came up with the idea for this special tour, but you can't control things.

That's been one of my biggest lessons in my life, and I hope you learn it faster than your hardheaded aunt! So many times I've wanted to be in charge of my life, forgetting that God has His own plans for me. When I was much younger, I planned to be a missionary. When your uncle didn't share that dream, I was devastated. Little did I know that God's plan for me was to do my mission work later in life. And I'm so glad I waited! Not only did I get to enjoy a wonderful marriage to a man I loved, but now I am here with the wisdom that comes with age. I am a better missionary now than I would've been back then. I didn't know it at the time, but God did.

So, darling Cheryl, remember what it says in Proverbs 19:21, "Many are the plans in a person's heart, but it is the Lord's purpose that prevails."

Give my love to Naomi and her sweet family. And tell Ben and Rueben that I said hello and that I've taught some of the natives how to play checkers thanks to a recent care package I received. It didn't have a name, but I have an idea of who sent it.

One final thing—go easy on Richard Wellaby. He's had his share of heartache. That is no excuse for the way he treats others, but you must know he is one of the "walking wounded" and hasn't figured out that God heals those wounds.

Keep me posted on your missing bus! I'm praying for you always.

Much love,
Aunt Mitzi

Cheryl closed her laptop and pondered Aunt Mitzi's words. It was always amazing to Cheryl that more times than not, Aunt Mitzi's letters and e-mails gave her advice at the exact time she needed it. Many times, Cheryl had been guilty of trying to control things around her rather than praying that God would show her His plan.

Just like with the tour bus. She'd been so caught up in finding it and so sure she could do a better job than the authorities. Maybe she needed to take a step back and accept that the outcome was in God's hands. And capable hands they were.

Lacey walked into the living room with a towel on her head. "I smelled a little like a goat, so I figured I'd better take a shower tonight." She grinned. "That is a very cool place the Millers have. I'd love to come back when it's not so cold and see the petting zoo and corn maze in action."

"You definitely should make plans to do that."

Lacey plopped down on the couch and pulled her legs into a cross-legged position. Even in yoga pants and an oversized University of Alabama hoodie, she managed to look like she belonged in a magazine. "Okay, spill it." She looked at Cheryl expectantly.

"What do you mean?" Cheryl asked. She felt frumpy in her purple and gray flannel pajamas next to Lacey.

"Oh, come on! You and Levi. There's totally some kind of vibe there."

Cheryl knew her normal reaction would be to deny. But she'd become friends with Lacey. She wanted to tell her the complete truth. "I think there is a vibe. But at the same time, I don't know that it matters much."

"Why? He's totally cute, and the two of you look like you genuinely enjoy one another."

"It's complicated."

"Try me." Lacey held up her hand and inspected her nails. "In fact, tell me your story. I know you mentioned that you had a fiancé once. But you didn't tell me what happened to him."

Cheryl shrugged. "Lance and I were engaged for five years. In the end, he decided he didn't want to get married."

"Yikes. That's terrible. But are you at the point now where you know you're better off without him?"

"Oh, definitely. You want to hear something crazy? He came to see me right before Christmas and tried to get back together. But that certainly wasn't even an option for me."

"Because you'd already met Levi?"

Cheryl blushed. "Levi really didn't have anything to do with it. But I will admit that in the back of my mind, I did consider that there were guys out there like him. You know? With the qualities that I've always hoped to find in a husband."

"*Like* him, huh? But *not* him?" Lacey flashed a mischievous smile. "Whatever you say. What kind of qualities though?"

"Besides the obvious—handsome and nice, you mean?" Cheryl grinned. "He's a man of his word. I trust him. He has a strong faith in God. And family means everything to him. He treats everyone with kindness." Her face grew hot as she heard herself practically deeming

Levi the perfect man. "But there are complications that prevent me from even considering it. He's Amish. I'm not. For us to ever be together, something major would have to happen." She thought of Richard and Lottie. Were she and Levi destined for that same path of heartbreak if they allowed their relationship to grow any closer?

Lacey nodded. "I've done a little research, believe it or not. I wasn't sure I'd be able to come on the Live Like the Amish tour, so I bought this *Amish Made Simple* book." She laughed. "I know, that sounds super odd. But I learned some stuff, and I even read a little bit about marrying outside of the Amish faith. I can see that there'd be some challenges there."

Just when Cheryl thought she had Lacey all pegged as just a pop star with an extravagant lifestyle, she surprised her. "To say 'challenges' is really an understatement."

"'The course of true love never did run smooth.'" As soon as Lacey caught sight of Cheryl's face, she laughed. "I'm not saying you love him. I'm just saying it's been my experience that some of the best things in life aren't exactly the easy things. Anything worthwhile usually takes work."

Cheryl nodded. "It's a moot point anyway. Levi would never cross that line. He's much too honorable. Ooh. Honor. That's another one to add to that list of qualities."

Lacey burst out laughing. "Okay. Whatever you say. I'll accept that you guys are just friends, but I still say you're missing the boat by not acting on those feelings that I know you have."

It was easy for a girl like Lacey to encourage acting on feelings. She was perfect. From her long, shiny dark hair to her full lips, to her petite size-four figure. But for Cheryl, it wasn't that simple. As much as she hated to admit it, Lance had shaken her confidence. And though she was getting it back slowly and surely, she wasn't quite there yet.

But something about the way Levi looked at her gave her hope and made her happy.

And for now, that was enough.

Chapter Twenty-Two

Sunday morning, Cheryl woke to the sound of rain. For a long moment, she burrowed deeper underneath her covers and enjoyed the warmth. Then she smelled it. Bacon. Even on a cold and rainy morning, bacon could get her out of bed.

She slipped on her comfy slippers and pulled her robe around her then padded down the hall to the kitchen.

Lacey stood at the stove, quilted apron over a dress that looked years too mature for her age.

"That smells amazing," Cheryl said. "And from the looks of that dress, I'm guessing I'll be attending church with a granny friend?"

Lacey giggled. "I love bacon, and it's one of those things that's not exactly on my daily diet. The sizzle, the smell—it reminds me of summertime at Nana's. She'd make bacon and eggs—the farm-fresh kind, plus pancakes. It was divine."

Cheryl poured herself a cup of coffee. "Well thanks for cooking. I guess I stayed in bed a little too long this morning."

"I can't blame you. This cold weather is good for sleeping, that's for sure." She expertly flipped the bacon on to a waiting paper-towel-covered plate. "And yes, you'll be attending church with a granny today if that's okay." A dark cloud passed over Lacey's face.

"Everything okay?"

Lacey set the bacon on the table next to the crescent rolls she'd already placed there then took a seat. "Well, it's kind of been a long time since I've set foot inside a church."

"It's okay. Silo Church is a very welcoming place. I promise no one will meet you at the door to inquire about your church attendance habits."

That brought a smile to Lacey's face, albeit a small one. "I never meant to be in this place. When I was a little girl, I was so involved in my church. I grew up in the Bible belt, after all. I spent summers at church camp and Vacation Bible School. I had a youth group, and we did work camps and all that stuff. I started out singing in the church choir."

Cheryl had read a little about Lacey's church choir days in a *People* magazine. "So what happened?"

"Did you ever have something happen that shook you to the core? Like really shook your faith?"

Cheryl took a sip of her coffee and thought for a moment. "My dad is a pastor at a big church in Seattle. And even though you may have heard horror stories about preachers' kids, I never really struggled with it. I wasn't a rebel or anything. I guess I had a pretty calm and uneventful adolescence. I watched my friends struggle with their faith at times, but I always felt like God was my greatest comforter."

"I did okay as long as I was surrounded by my family and friends who'd grown up just like me." Lacey chewed thoughtfully on a slice of bacon. "But as soon as my faith was tested, I turned my back on it. And I knew better."

"What happened?"

"It seems so cliché to blame it on a tragedy. But when I was eighteen, my dad was killed in a car accident. I sort of lost it. I blamed God and wanted nothing to do with Him. It was about the same time I was beginning to see a little success. It seemed like the farther away from my faith I got, the more successful I became. I sometimes wonder if that wasn't something that happened on purpose a little." She sighed. "Because the more success I saw, the easier it was to just leave the person I had been and become someone else entirely. I'm not proud of it."

Cheryl was sure she'd read the story of Lacey's father—something about falling asleep at the wheel after a long trip. "I'm so sorry about your dad. And I feel certain you can still find your way back. Maybe today at the Silo Church, dressed like a little old lady, you can start to figure out the way."

"Let's hope so. Last night, watching the Millers pray for their food, I realized that my life has been lacking for such a long time. That prayer kapp I've been wearing has made me more conscious of how much I crave a relationship with God again." She smiled. "It seems silly, but just having the kapp on my head was like a constant reminder to pray. And now that I've become accustomed to that, I don't want to go back to the way I was before I came here."

"Does that mean you're going to continue to wear the kapp?" Cheryl teased.

Lacey grinned. "Ja. For the next couple of months anyway. But only on set."

Two hours later, Cheryl pulled her Ford Focus into the church parking lot. "Ready for this?"

"As ready as I'll ever be." Lacey smoothed her gray wig and squared her shoulders. "It's time for me to get back to where I need to be."

"Did I see Roy in the back of the church?" Cheryl asked later as they got back in the vehicle. "Wonder why he didn't stay to talk."

"He texted me earlier to say that he was going to have to dash out as soon as church was over. He's headed to Columbus to his office for a few hours. He's having computer issues here and is going to exchange his laptop for a different one. He said he'd be back soon." She sighed. "He may not be able to take me to Dover today after all."

"I'm sorry." Cheryl could see Lacey's disappointment. "How about lunch to cheer you up? The Sunday buffet at the Alpine Kitchen restaurant is fantastic." She smiled. "And I meant it when I said I'd drive you back to Dover today—or you can borrow my car."

Lacey brightened. "The buffet sounds fabulous. I guess I'll be going back to my diet soon. And if you're sure you don't mind, I think I would like to borrow it for just a bit. I'd really like to spend some more time with my grandparents before I have to leave tomorrow." She flipped through her phone. "This is so weird."

"What is?" Cheryl was about at her limit with weird, what with the missing bus and the faux Miller family that Roy's grandma had mentioned yesterday—not to mention Michael Rogers's intentions and the two men who'd been following Lacey. The whole weekend was weird with a capital *W*.

"It's a text from a number I'm not familiar with. But it's obviously to me. It's the same guy who texted me Friday." She shook her head. "I only give this number to people I trust completely."

It dawned on Cheryl that she hadn't even been provided with Lacey's personal cell number. "Oh?"

Lacey glanced over at her. "Like literally only a handful of people. My nana, Blake, my dog sitter, my assistant, and now Roy." She grinned. "I haven't gotten around to giving it to you yet, but I totally will."

"What does the text say?" Cheryl pulled into the crowded parking lot at the Alpine Kitchen restaurant.

"'*I wanted to talk to you the other day, but those mean-looking guys ran me off. I saw you again the next day, but I didn't know whether to say anything. I didn't want to scare you. Sorry about visiting your grandparents. I was hoping you would be there, but your grandma didn't even know you were in town. I got your number and thought it might be easier this way. I'll be in touch soon.*'" Lacey made a face. "Does that sound scary *stalkery* to you or just regular *stalkery*?"

Cheryl hadn't had much experience in the stalker department. "I think maybe let's just focus on how this person would've gotten your number."

"But no one who has my number would give it out. So that's the part that's a little nerve-racking."

They went up the steps to the restaurant and into the foyer where a few guests stood waiting to be seated. Cheryl put their name on the list for a table and walked back to where Lacey stood. "Maybe it was an honest mistake. Maybe this is someone who knows one of those people you listed and they got the number when they weren't looking. Although, that's kind of creepy." She sighed. "Maybe it's someone who works for the phone company."

"I didn't even register it in my name. My assistant did."

Cheryl raised an eyebrow. Just when she and Lacey seemed to have so much in common, it dawned on her that in many ways their lives were nothing alike. Lacey had a personal assistant to do all those errands and chores that most people had to fit in between work and sleep. "Maybe the mystery texter knows you?"

Lacey shrugged. "The e-mail and text both reference that he saw me. We know he followed me at least twice since I've been here. He even went to see my grandparents. That isn't public information. I've tried hard to keep Nana and Papa out of the news."

"But if someone wanted to dig around and find them, they could."

"Well, yeah. But why would anyone do that?"

The hostess called them to their table, and they both ordered the buffet.

"Fried chicken, mashed potatoes, rolls... This looks so amazing." Lacey's eyes widened at the row of freshly cooked food. "I'm even skipping the salad and going right for the good stuff." She spooned a serving of gravy over her potatoes. "It kind of reminds me of church potluck when I was a little kid."

Cheryl laughed. "I guess so."

They ate in silence for several minutes, then Lacey's phone buzzed. She gingerly picked it up. "It's the same number as earlier." She peered at the screen. "*'I'll be in touch soon, and we can catch up. Can't wait.*'" Lacey's face grew white. "That can't be good."

"Text back. Ask who it is."

Lacey shook her head. "Blake always told me not to engage with these kind of people. He says it's best to just ignore them and that eventually they'll move on. Of course, sometimes he reports the incidents for me. Phone records, stuff like that." She shrugged. "I'm not going to worry about it for now. But we need to be on the lookout for that white car. This sounds like he's getting ready to try and actually make contact."

"Of course." What would it be like to have to constantly look over her shoulder? Cheryl hoped she never had to find out. "But I still say you might want to text back. Or I could do it from my phone. Those messages don't really sound threatening. In fact, they almost sound like they think you know who they are." She spooned some gravy over her mashed potatoes. "Maybe you should call Roy and fill him in too."

Lacey shrugged. "I'll call Blake when we leave here and fill him in. He may want to get the number and talk to the police. Just to be sure it's all on record."

"Sounds like a plan." Cheryl drizzled honey butter on a hot biscuit then took a bite. Pure bliss. "How about we do some sightseeing today when you get back from Dover? If Roy's not back, I mean. I know y'all drove around some yesterday, but I'm sure there are lots of sights you haven't seen yet."

"Okay." Lacey nodded. "Tomorrow I head back home. My flight is late in the afternoon." She widened her eyes. "I was supposed to be on the tour bus back to the airport. Wonder what's going to happen."

Cheryl had no idea. She'd just have to pray it all worked out. Somehow.

Chapter Twenty-Three

"What's been your favorite part?" Cheryl asked later that afternoon. Lacey had spent a couple of hours visiting her grandparents, then Cheryl had taken her to see all there was to see in Sugarcreek and the surrounding area.

"I still can't get over seeing the buggies everywhere. Horse-and-buggy parking at the McDonald's… That cracks me up." Lacey grinned. "And I thought it was pretty cool to drive past those houses and see the Amish kids playing outside. I'm not sure kids today play outside that much, but I guess here they do."

"Not having a television or video games inside helps."

"Think of how much more connected we'd all be to one another if no home had a television or an Xbox. I mean, we'd have to actually *talk*." Lacey grinned. "I think they may be on to something actually. Sometimes I think my constant connection to technology makes my life extra stressful. I check my phone before I fall asleep, and then when my eyes are barely open in the morning, I reach for my phone. Sometimes if I get up in the middle of the night, I check it then too." She shuddered. "It took seeing people function normally without a phone glued to their hand to make me realize that I may be missing out on life, always looking at it through a phone camera and Instagram filter."

"Don't beat yourself up. Most of us are guilty of that." It was true. Cheryl wasn't as glued to her phone as she had been when she'd lived in Columbus, but she still had her moments where she had to remind herself to connect to the people in front of her and not just the ones on the screen. "If there's nowhere else you want to stop, I'm going to head to the cottage. Beau must be feeling neglected."

"Sounds good." Lacey yawned. "What a nice day. Although you know, I'm starting to get a little worried that we aren't going to find this bus and all those people before tomorrow. When that happens, all their families are going to be here. This is going to be a huge story—can you imagine all the reporters?" She shook her head. "I mean, bus full of elderly tourists goes missing in Ohio Amish country. It sounds like the plot of a Lifetime movie."

"Well, once this whole ordeal is over, maybe you can play the star," Cheryl said. "But until then, we just have to stay determined that we find them." She sighed. "I don't feel like cooking tonight. Do you want to stop and pick something up?"

Lacey grinned. "Roy may be back in time to take me out for a late dinner. But I'd love to stop back by Swiss Village Market. I'm dying for another fry pie, and they had some amazing-looking cookies. Plus, I can't get enough of the cheese. I think my new favorite is that smoky flavor. I may move here just for the cheese."

Cheryl laughed. "I suppose there are worse reasons to relocate." She headed through town toward Swiss Village Market.

"Do you think you'll stay in Sugarcreek? Like permanently?" Lacey asked.

Cheryl had asked herself the same question a few times over the months. "I love it here. The town embraced me. I've made so many good friends—Naomi and her whole family—"

"Yeah, Levi," Lacey interrupted.

Cheryl smiled. "Levi. But also Esther and Elizabeth and the rest of them. I'm attached to Ben and Rueben and watching their relationship be mended through their checkers games. The Berryhills have become friends, as have the Swartzentrubers. Kathy Snyder is a great friend. And there are so many others."

"It's nice to have true friends. The kind you can count on no matter what." Lacey sighed. "It makes me think of that Amish proverb on the back of that receipt. You can't put a price on a good friend who will step in and help you when you need it."

"You sure can't. That's one thing I like about living here. Plus, I've come to love the slower pace. I've also found a church home that makes me feel like I belong. And I really enjoy running the Swiss Miss. So yeah, I guess I can honestly say that I plan on staying in Sugarcreek."

"Do I hear a 'but' in there somewhere?"

Cheryl laughed. "I think it was God's plan for me to be here in the first place. Whether it's His plan for me to remain here for the rest of my life remains to be seen. So I guess I can safely say that I'm not looking to go anywhere, but you just never know what might be in store."

"I like that." Lacey leaned her head back against the seat. She pushed a gray curl from her eye. "I've been thinking a lot about my life. It's so easy to get swept up in things that don't really matter and turn your back on the important things."

"Sounds like your time in Sugarcreek, though chaotic, has been a good reflective time."

"It sure has. I guess there are pieces of me that I've kept hidden from the world—particularly my faith—that I don't want to hide any longer. When I get back to my 'real life,' I want to use that platform I've been given. Without God's blessings I wouldn't be where I am today, and I need to share that sentiment with the world."

Cheryl was struck by the authenticity in Lacey's words. "Just like Aunt Mitzi is a missionary overseas—I guess you'll sort of be one too."

"Aren't we all supposed to be though? I mean, really?" Lacey asked. "In some way, shouldn't we all be missionaries? Even if it's just in our own communities?"

"Yes, I believe you're right." Cheryl pulled into the parking lot at Swiss Village Market. "Is it okay if I wait in the car? I don't think I really want anything."

"You sure? I'll grab a pineapple fry pie for you." Lacey grinned. "Just in case you get hungry later."

"Well, I guess that would be okay." Cheryl smiled as Lacey bounded out of the car. She had mastered the "little old lady" shuffle, but when she was excited about something, her gait reverted back to normal.

Twenty minutes later, Cheryl was beginning to get restless. What was taking so long? Had Lacey decided to sample the whole store? She finally spotted her exiting the building, two bags in hand and a dour expression on her face.

"I hate standing in line," Lacey grumbled when she got in the car. "I ended up behind this guy with his foot in one of those boot things—you know like if you have a sprain or something. Anyway, he was buying all these fry pies in different flavors. He thought he'd counted wrong, so he asked me to count them. Twenty-four. Who needs twenty-four fry pies in different flavors? I mean, come on."

Cheryl's ears perked up. "Hold on. Twenty-four is the number of people on our tour bus. That's the number of coffees that were purchased the other morning from the coffee shop. And that's the number of cheese samplers that were purchased and on that receipt left in your bag."

Cheryl and Lacey stared at one another for a long moment, wide eyed.

"Did you recognize the man?"

"Never seen him before in my life."

"Has he left yet?"

Lacey peered around the parking lot. "There he is! Just getting into his old truck."

Cheryl watched as the battered old green Chevy's lights came on. "That's an old model. Surprised it still runs."

"Didn't Lydia's brother see an old green truck parked at the phone shed?" Lacey asked excitedly.

Cheryl nodded. "It's got to be the same truck."

"So should we follow him?" Lacey asked.

"Definitely." Both Roy and Twitchell had implored that she not snoop around on her own, and she figured having Lacey along as an accomplice wasn't what either of them had in mind. "Call Roy and tell him what's going on."

"It's just like my made-for-TV movie, *Telltale Truck*. There was this truck spotted at the scene of a crime, and later my character saw it and trailed the bad guy to his hideout."

"How did that turn out?"

"Well, I got kidnapped and ended up almost getting eaten by an alligator. So maybe this won't turn out like the movie."

Cheryl pulled out of the parking lot behind the man in the Chevy, her nerves tingling.

"Roy's not answering. It's going to his voice mail."

"Well just wait a minute. We'll call him once we see where this guy is headed." Cheryl slowed the car. She should probably back off so the man wouldn't realize he was being followed.

Lacey eyed her phone. "Let's just hope my signal stays strong. I'm down to one bar." She held the phone up toward the ceiling.

What a time for technology to fail. "Yeah, that's a real possibility. We're headed toward Charm, which is a very small Amish community. You should begin to see the signs for Keim Lumber Company soon." Cheryl had visited the large lumber company a few months ago and had been amazed, both at the size and the selection. It was quite an impressive store for such a tiny community. But Keim did business all over the country, even having selections of specialty wood that were hard to find elsewhere.

The pickup truck's brake lights shone in the distance, but an SUV went around Cheryl. "I can't see him now, but I think he's still in front of this SUV." She squinted. "It looks like he's going around a buggy."

Cheryl was on the SUV's tail, and the driver tapped on the brakes. "Guess I'm a little close." She slowed.

"I don't see the truck anymore," Lacey said. "I had him in sight till he went around that buggy. Now it seems like he's disappeared." She sighed. "This is just great. We totally had him and now... *poof*. He's gone just like that tour bus."

Cheryl shared in her frustrations. "Let's just head back to the cottage. At least we have a general direction. And if he was shopping at Swiss Village Market, our busload can't be that far from here." She pulled into a driveway and turned the car around then headed back toward Sugarcreek.

They rode in silence, rendered mute by the disappointment of losing sight of the truck.

Cheryl greeted Beau when they walked into the house. She wanted nothing more than to take a hot shower then curl up in her cozy bed with Beau and a good book.

"That's weird," Lacey said. She held up her bag from Swiss Village Market. "Looks like I came home with an extra bag. I guess there was one left behind on the carousel and I grabbed it along with mine." She pulled two raisin fry pies from the bag and wrinkled her nose. "I definitely didn't buy these. Raisin pie sounds disgusting." She pulled out a bottle and set it on the coffee table. "Or this. I totally don't do tan from a bottle. Spray booth, yes; bottle, no. Always turns me orange."

Cheryl stopped in her tracks. Maybe curling up with a good book would have to wait. "Do you think this bag was one left behind by the guy in the boot?"

"No way to know. But it seems like that's the most reasonable explanation. He bought all those pies, and they were in different flavors." Lacey looked at her curiously. "Why? Do you have some kind of idea where he may be?"

"Maybe." Cheryl racked her brain. It made no sense, but it was all she had to go on. "I think we should go back out. I'd like to stop in at the Raber homestead to see if my hunch is right."

"Ooh! Do you think the group is there? And why?"

Cheryl explained about Velma and her orangey appearance. "It is probably a long shot. But we don't have anything to lose."

"Okay. Hang on. Let me grab that coat and hat. It's getting cold out there." She giggled. "If we see Roy, he may mistake me for his grandma." She pulled on the purple cape and hat. "Let's go."

They told Beau bye and got back in the car.

"Do you want me to call him again?" Lacey asked.

Cheryl nodded. "Please do."

Lacey dialed Roy's number. "Ugh. Voice mail again. I can't believe he's not back."

"Call back and leave him a message. Tell him he'll need to go get Naomi and have her take him to the old Raber place. The one that used to be the Christmas tree farm."

Lacey did as Cheryl asked. "I sent him a text too, just in case." She squirmed in the seat. "Are you nervous? I'm a little nervous."

"Not exactly. More like excited. I don't think we're walking into anything dangerous. I just want to figure out once and for all what's going on." If Cheryl was correct about who was holding the tour group captive, she really didn't think they had anything to worry about. Although, she supposed some people could be unbalanced and manage to put forth a totally normal appearance. Look at all those serial killers. "Well, maybe a little nervous." She slowed down and pulled over on the side of the road. "That's the driveway to the farmhouse." She pointed to the gravel road. "I don't want to pull in because they might see my lights. Plus if I park here, Roy will definitely see the car." She met Lacey's skeptical gaze. "He'll come for us. I feel sure he won't let missed calls from *you* go unanswered for too long." At least she hoped not.

Lacey didn't say anything for a long moment.

"What? Do you think we should just wait for Roy to get here?" Cheryl hoped against hope that Lacey would say no. She pushed that whole "serial killer" thing out of her mind.

"I guess that would be the responsible thing to do." Lacey held up her phone. "Except that he's not answering my calls or texts."

"True."

"How about Chief Twitch?"

Cheryl laughed. "Twitchell. And I'm not sure about calling him. This may very well be a wild goose chase. We have nothing concrete, and if we raise a false alarm with him, I'll just feel stupid."

Lacey giggled. "I get the feeling you and old Twitchell aren't exactly the best of friends."

"He seems to feel like I've interfered with one too many of his investigations since I moved here. I've tried to explain to him that I just seem to be in the right place at the right time, but he doesn't buy it." She grinned. "And here we go again. You sure you don't want to wait for Roy?"

Lacey peered over her old-lady bifocals at Cheryl. "Nope. He's not picking up. So I guess it's up to you and me, dearie," she said in her feeble, elderly voice. "We'll have to save the day ourselves."

Cheryl grinned. "Okay then. Are you ready?"

Lacey nodded. "I've got my trusty purple cape and hat. I'm like a geriatric superhero." She got out of the car and swished her cape then posed with her hands on her hips.

"You look like one, that's for sure. And I'm sure Roy's granny will be happy to know you've used her discarded hat and coat as a costume."

"I'll just tell her she contributed to my disguise and helped to keep me safe. Surely she'll understand." Lacey shivered. "Besides, it's getting so cold. I wasn't really prepared for any nighttime *detectiving* when I packed for the weekend. I was thinking more along the lines of hot chocolate and a good book by a warm fire."

They set off down the long driveway. Without street lights to guide them, it was extra dark. "It's so dark and quiet out here that it's almost eerie. The city is never this quiet." Lacey pulled the cape around her, shivering. "Not to mention that it gets cold fast when the sun goes down."

"Not much farther. We'll just see if we notice anything in the windows of the farmhouse ahead. I've driven past the driveway a few times, and the place has always looked pretty deserted."

They crept around the barn and saw the green pickup truck in the driveway.

"Come over here," Cheryl whispered. "I think there's someone in the living room."

The two of them slowly made their way to the side of the house. "I'll take this window," Cheryl whispered, pointing toward the front. "You take the one at the side. Meet me back here once you've had a chance to look."

Cheryl bent down and approached the nearest window. She slowly raised up until she could see over the ledge. She gasped then clasped her hand over her mouth.

She'd found her missing tour group.

Chapter Twenty-Four

Cheryl still couldn't believe her eyes. Several members of the Live Like the Amish tour group were in the living room, and a man she'd never seen before was passing out fry pies. He must be the one who'd been in front of Lacey at the grocery store because he had a walking boot on his foot. She watched for a few more minutes. The group was laughing and talking, exclaiming over each bite of their pies. It didn't make any sense. She crept to the next window and slowly raised up. Mickey Simmons and three other men were putting together what looked like a handmade wooden trunk. Mickey appeared to be the leader of the group, showing the others what to do. So Mickey had been involved after all. Naomi would be upset.

She crept back to the side of the house and waited for Lacey.

"Did you see anything?" Lacey hissed.

Cheryl nodded. "Did you?"

"Yes." Lacey motioned toward the barn. "Let's go in there and figure out what to do."

They slowly made their way to the barn, and Cheryl opened the door. Once they were inside, she used the flashlight app on her phone to look around. She spotted a lantern in the corner and lit it. The barn was pretty dim, but at least now they could look around.

Paint and brushes sat in the corner, along with several wadded-up drop cloths. Several new fence slats were stacked against the nearest stall. "Looks like someone is renovating," she observed. She quickly filled Lacey in on what she'd seen.

"Fry-pie tasting? Woodworking?" Lacey shook her head. "Those are all things that you advertised for the tour. It almost seems like someone just took the tour and moved it here instead of where it was supposed to be."

"What did you see?" Cheryl asked. "Anything interesting?"

"There were people sitting around a table, and I'm sure they were some of the ladies from the tour. It looked like they were quilting. There was a woman who looked very familiar. I think maybe she's the one you were talking about who was in your store the other day. Kind of on the petite side. Blond hair that is definitely from a bottle."

Velma? It had to be. "Was she a little too tanned for these parts in January?"

"Kind of orangey actually, although not like the other day." Lacey grinned. "You were right. The self-tanner must've been for her. So Velma and Mickey worked together to bring the group here. But why? Why would any of this be happening?" Lacey asked. "None of it makes sense. The people looked like they were actually on the Live Like the Amish tour that you planned."

"What should we do now? Leave and go get Roy? Confront them ourselves?" Cheryl wasn't sure how best to handle the situation.

The barn door burst open behind them.

"Freeze, Granny," a familiar voice said.

Cheryl turned to see none other than Riggins and McGraw closing in on Lacey. They each had a gun pointed right at her.

"Hand it over," Riggins barked. "And no one gets hurt."

Lacey slowly turned toward them with her hands up. "Hand what over?"

"You know what we want. The lipstick. Just hand over the lipstick, and we'll be out of your hair."

Lacey's face went pale. She shuffled through her purse that she'd worn across her body and pulled out three lipstick tubes. "H...Here you go," she said. "You can have them all. I have more if you'll give me time to dig around."

Riggins let out a growl. "Don't play around with us, Granny. You know what I'm talking about."

Granny? Of course. Lacey was using Roy's granny's clothes as her disguise today. In the dimly lit barn, the two men must think they'd found the real thing.

"I really don't know what you mean," Lacey began. "This is all the lipstick I have."

As the men continued to focus on Lacey, Cheryl spotted a shovel leaned against a stall. She crept toward it, wondering if she could really hit someone upside the head with a shovel if the need arose. Maybe if it meant life or death. Other than that, she wasn't altogether sure she could do it.

Riggins pointed the gun straight at Lacey. "Last chance, Granny. Give me the lipstick."

It definitely seemed like life or death. Cheryl had to do something. She grabbed the shovel and reared back. She'd take them by surprise.

The cow whose stall she was next to chose that moment to moo loudly.

McGraw was on her in a flash. "Drop it, lady." He roughly grabbed her arm and pulled her over to where Lacey stood trembling.

"Please. No one needs to get hurt." Cheryl tried to keep her voice calm, but her words came out wobbly. Kind of like her knees. "You've got the wrong person. She's not Granny."

The barn door burst open with a clang. Cheryl and Lacey used the distraction to run to the other side of the barn, but Riggins was too fast.

Roy jumped on him just as the gun fired.

Cheryl let out a scream before she hit the ground as Lacey tackled her.

And everything went black.

"Cheryl?"

She opened her eyes. Lacey hovered over her, gray wig askew. "Is anyone dead?"

"No, silly. I'm sorry I knocked you down. I thought that guy was going to take us both out." Lacey grinned. "I forgot to mention that I do my own stunts. But I didn't mean to hit you so hard."

Cheryl sat up slowly and glanced around. Roy had the faux detectives in cuffs and was talking to them. Velma, Mickey, and most of the tour group watched curiously from the barn door. Naomi stepped inside the barn and hurried toward Cheryl and Lacey.

"You're bleeding," Cheryl said, noticing the blood on Lacey's arm.

Lacey lifted her arm. "I guess I scraped it against a nail or something. If this story hits the papers though, it'll probably declare that I was grazed with a bullet. Ooh, maybe they'll call me a hero for throwing myself on top of you to save you from certain death."

Near-death experience and she was still as dramatic as ever. Cheryl grinned. "What was it you called yourself earlier? Geriatric Super Girl?"

Lacey struck her superhero pose. "Sounds good to me."

"I'm so glad Roy arrived in time," Naomi said as she reached them. "He came by the house and got me as soon as he heard your voice mail." She smiled. "Levi and Seth stayed behind, but I think they were sorely tempted to come and see what was going on."

She knelt down beside Cheryl. "Are you okay?"

Cheryl nodded and stood up. Her body would ache in the morning. The older she got, the more bumps and bruises hurt. Thirty wasn't bad, but she knew a hot bath was in order when she got home. "I'm a little bruised, but I'll be fine."

The door burst open and Chief Twitchell and one of his deputies stormed in, each with a prisoner. "Is everyone okay in here?" the chief asked gruffly.

"Michael Rogers!" Cheryl exclaimed. Twitchell's deputy had Michael by the arm.

"Blake?" Lacey asked. She ran over to Chief Twitchell. "What is he doing here?"

Twitchell frowned. "That's what I'm trying to figure out. These two were sneaking away from the barn windows as we came up the drive. I thought they may be in cahoots with these other two bozos, but it seems like they're unrelated."

Cheryl glared at Michael. "I knew you weren't in town for a vacation. Why were you really here?"

Michael looked sheepish. "I'm a director. I'm hoping to get a reality series sold that's set in Amish country." He turned his gaze to Lacey. "You probably don't remember me, but we worked together when you first got to Hollywood. I directed one of your music videos."

"You've been following me this week." Lacey kept her glare pointed toward Blake. "And Blake helped you."

"Lacey, babe, I was just trying to keep you on your toes. Michael is an old friend of mine, and he wanted to reach out to you. I thought this way we could have a little fun with the media. They love a good stalker story. And you played your part well. Those frantic texts you sent me were perfect. I sent screen shots to several media outlets this morning. By tonight, the whole world will fear for your safety."

"What do I do with these two?" Twitchell asked Roy.

"You don't even want to know what I want you to do with them," Roy growled. "It would be far too unpleasant."

"I'd like a word with them. Outside." Lacey stormed out of the barn, followed quickly by Michael and Blake.

Naomi glanced at Cheryl. "Are you okay? That cut needs to be tended to."

Cheryl shook her head. "I'm fine. I think I want to have a little chat with Velma first."

She dusted herself off and walked to the barn door. Velma's eyes met hers. Her cheerful expression from their earlier meeting was gone, replaced by the look of defeat. Cheryl motioned to Velma. "Send the group back for dessert. I'd like to talk to you alone."

Velma, eyes full of tears, only nodded. A few minutes later, she joined Cheryl and Naomi.

"I'm so sorry," Velma began. "I know I shouldn't have done that."

"No. You shouldn't have." Cheryl kept her voice firm but kind. "We were very worried about those people. What is going on out here?"

Velma sighed. "It all started a few months ago. My aunt passed away, and her kids had long ago left the Amish faith. My cousins live in Florida now and have no interest in coming back here. Aunt Abigail always felt for me because I don't have any children of my own." Fresh tears splashed down Velma's round face.

"So what happened?" Naomi asked softly.

"She left the whole place to me. Patrick wasn't really enthused about moving here from California, but we were kind of in a tough spot there financially. So we figured maybe the cost of living here would make things easier." She sighed. "When we got here, the place was pretty much in shambles. Aunt Abigail had been having some local boys tend to the animals, but she'd let the place go. We knew as soon as we got here that we were in over our heads. We decided the best thing to do was to fix the place up a little and put it up for sale. With the profits, we could head back to a warmer climate." In spite of her tears, she managed a tiny smile. "We're not much for the cold."

Ohio in January must be a real shock to their systems. "I'm still confused about why you took over our tour group." Cheryl noticed Mickey standing in a corner of the barn, looking like a little boy waiting to see the principal. She'd deal with him in a minute.

"We were managing the renovations okay until Patrick fell and broke his foot. Then I had to do it all—care for the animals, work on the house—it's always something. It's been so much work for me to do alone." She motioned toward Mickey. "Mick would help me when he had days off, but even so, we couldn't get the job done."

Cheryl rubbed her head. Had she banged it harder than she thought? None of this was making sense. "Mickey?"

"Oh yeah. We've known Mickey for a long time. He used to live across the street from Patrick when they were kids. So we were glad to reconnect with him when we moved here."

Mickey joined the circle. "It's all my fault. The whole thing is my fault."

"This one." Velma shook her head. "This one felt so guilty I thought he was going to call you and confess as soon as he got here. And don't let him fool you. It's not his fault. It's mine."

"I'm still not following the part about how the tour bus ended up here—or why?"

"Oh, that." Velma sighed. "Well I overheard you and your Amish man friend talking about some of the tasks your group would be doing. Helping with the animals, mending the fence, stuff like that. And I thought, 'Oh, Velma. That's what you need. A whole army of people at your house wanting to help you do chores.' So I asked Mickey what he thought about it."

Mickey nodded toward Naomi. "Mrs. Naomi had already asked me if I was interested in driving the bus. She mentioned that the idea of the group sort of stressed her out. So I guess...I guess I kinda thought of it as if I were doing her a favor by bringing the group here."

Now it made sense. Or at least, Cheryl could see where they were coming from. "So you brought them here instead of to the Millers'. And then you just proceeded with the weekend as if they were where they were supposed to be?"

"Oh yes. The group doesn't know any differently. I found a couple from Millersburg who'd been extras in one of those Amish movies that was filmed near here. They had some Amish garb, and I hired them to be Mr. and Mrs. Miller. They loved it." Velma at least had the decency to look sheepish. "And those two don't have any idea there was anything odd going on. They just think they were hired to play a part."

Well that explained Roy's granny calling and telling him how lovely the Millers were. Instead of Naomi and Seth, she'd met a set of faux Millers who'd been hired to be lovely and authentic seeming. "I don't know what to say."

Tears dripped down Velma's face again. "I don't know anyone here except for Patrick and Mickey. And with Patrick laid up and Mickey only able to help me every now and then, I just needed help so badly. I didn't know what to do with the place by myself. If I'd had friends I could call on to help, I would have."

Cheryl felt for the woman. The house was large, not to mention the land and the animals. Trying to do just daily upkeep must have been difficult, let alone trying to do renovations and repairs. "It sounds like you were really in a tough position."

"I wanted to tell you Saturday when I came to the store," Velma said. "In fact, I kept trying to figure out how I could start the conversation. But I lost my nerve."

"Is this why you bought all that jam? For all of your guests?"

Velma nodded. "For their breakfast biscuits. They loved it." She managed a wobbly smile. "And you know what? I really enjoyed having a house full of people."

"I guess what I don't understand is how this was going to end." Cheryl was having a hard time staying mad at Velma and Mickey. Their actions seemed like they were made out of desperation, and they'd meant no harm to the group.

"Well, I was trying to talk Mickey into saying he'd received a note telling him the address for the weekend had changed." Velma elbowed Mickey. "But he didn't want to lie. He was starting to regret going along with the whole thing."

Mickey cleared his throat. "The truth is, there was a time when I was in a pretty bad financial situation. Patrick and Velma gave me a good-sized loan. My part in this made us even. And Naomi has always been so nice to me, I guess I convinced myself I was doing her a favor by keeping the group from her home."

Naomi patted his arm. "You did not need to worry about me, Mickey. I would have handled the group just fine."

The man seemed truly remorseful. "I'm sorry."

"You were my mysterious caller, weren't you?" Cheryl asked.

He nodded. "I didn't want you to worry. I've driven for the Troyers before when they needed to go to Columbus, and I knew their phone shanty stays unlocked. They're far enough out that I didn't figure anyone would see me." He frowned. "Till yesterday morning. I was going to try to give you a hint as to their whereabouts, but Thomas was headed out to the barn."

"And Lacey's bag?"

"No one claimed it. I looked through it to find some identification. I found her name in there on some paperwork and thought I'd better return it to you." He smiled for the first time. "I wanted to give you some kinda clue or something, but I was in Velma's car at the time. I found that receipt from Swiss Village Market and put it inside."

"What was that supposed to tell me, exactly?"

He shrugged. "Well, I reckon anyone who buys such good cheese for all twenty-four people can't mean to harm them."

She had to laugh at how pleased Lacey would be to hear that. Her theory had been correct. "I suppose you're right."

"Are we in trouble?" Velma asked quietly. "And if so, is it the jail kind of trouble or more the community-service variety?"

That really wasn't for her to say. She and Naomi looked at one another and shrugged.

"Cheryl?" Roy called. "Can you come here for a minute? There's someone you need to speak to."

She'd never been so happy for an interruption.

Chapter Twenty-Five

"You may remember my grandma from the other day," Roy said. He had his arm around the little gray-haired lady. She was wearing the same clothes she'd had on when Cheryl had first seen her, except this time she was missing her purple hat and cape. "This is my grandma, Ethyl."

"I sure do remember her." Cheryl smiled. "Nice to officially meet you. I'm Cheryl. I'm sorry for the way I practically pushed you onto that bus. If it hadn't been for that..." She trailed off. If it hadn't been for that, then Roy wouldn't be here to help her. If it hadn't been for that, she wouldn't have spent the past few days with Lacey. It never ceased to amaze her how one tiny action could set off more reactions than could be counted.

Ethyl shook her head. "Oh, don't apologize. This is the best weekend I've had in such a long time. We've worked on quilts and cared for farm animals. This morning I had the most delicious homemade bread and jam for breakfast. It's just been a real treat."

"I was trying to explain to Grandma that those weren't really the Millers."

"Well I don't care what their names are. They've been the most wonderful hosts. And that Velma, the activity director—she's been such a hoot."

Cheryl was more conflicted than ever. "It all sounds wonderful." In fact, it all sounded just like she'd planned, except that she'd imagined the group about ten miles down the road from here.

"I'm hoping this will be a yearly event," Ethyl said. "Or maybe even seasonal. Mrs. Miller was telling me how beautiful the flowers are in the spring and the leaves in the fall. I hope you'll consider it."

It was all Cheryl could do to keep from laughing out loud. She couldn't wait to tell Levi that their tour had been a smashing success even though the bus had ended up missing for the better part of three days. "I'm so glad you enjoyed it. We'll certainly keep those thoughts in mind."

Once Ethyl went back to the group, Roy pulled Cheryl aside. "What did you learn from the homeowner?"

Cheryl quickly filled him in on what Velma and Mickey had told her. "She seemed so lost, so desperate. I get the feeling if she had friends and family around to help her, she would've just asked for help. I doubt she can afford to hire the kind of help a place of this size requires, so when her husband broke his foot and was out of commission, I'm sure she kind of broke down." She shrugged. "I know what she and Mickey did was wrong, but I really hate to punish them in any way, especially after hearing what a wonderful time your grandma has been having. It seems like they've really bent over backward to make sure the expectations of the group were met and everyone had a memorable time."

Roy smiled. "I'm inclined to agree. It seems like Chief Twitchell is more concerned with the two men we captured tonight. I feel like I can convince him that a stern warning to Velma and Mickey will be enough punishment for them. After all, I don't see this as something they will do again in the future."

"I agree completely."

Roy hesitated. "But what about tonight? Do you want to just leave them where they are? Or move them to the *real* Millers' house?"

"I think moving them tonight would just disrupt things even more. Most of the group has no idea what's going on. Their stuff is already here and their bedding is set up upstairs and I'm assuming in the empty *dawdy haus*." She hadn't asked Velma what the set up was, but that had been the plan at Naomi's and Seth's, to use their grandparents' house as well as vacant bedrooms upstairs in the main house.

"You can go confirm that with Velma." Roy's face broke into a broad smile as Lacey joined them.

It would be nice to be the reason someone's face lit up like that. Watching the spark this weekend between Lacey and Roy had really made Cheryl consider her own life. Sure, she enjoyed spending time hanging out with Levi, but would that ever really go anywhere? Like she'd told Lacey last night, it was complicated. But was she ready to date again? Even if she found the perfect guy, had she moved on from the hurts of the past? Only time would tell.

The barn door opened, and Blake stood at the entrance. "Lacey? Please don't be like that. Just hear me out."

Lacey's jaw tightened. "I've heard enough."

Roy placed a protective arm around her. "Do you want me to make him leave?"

She sighed. "Actually it's okay. I need to deal with this once and for all. I'll be back in a few."

She walked out, leaving Cheryl and Roy staring after her.

Roy looked at Cheryl with raised eyebrows.

Cheryl shrugged her shoulders. "Seems like her manager wasn't looking after her own interests after all. Let's hope she has enough backbone to send him packing."

Thirty minutes later, Cheryl and Roy had things settled with Velma and the tour group. They were going to leave the group with Velma. They were obviously in safe hands, and there was no reason to cause alarm now.

"I'll bring the group by the Swiss Miss tomorrow, I promise." Mickey's voice was still shaky. His remorse was causing him so much pain that Cheryl felt for him.

"Thanks, Mickey. Even though this has been a worrisome situation, I can see that you meant no harm. And thank you for making sure I knew the group was safe."

He gave her a small smile. "Thank you for not being too angry. I was just desperate. I had no way to pay them back the money I owed them. And they needed help in such a big way."

"Next time, just ask for help," Naomi said. She'd been standing in the background quietly listening to the explanations. "We are your friends, Mickey. We would have helped as much as we could to get your friends taken care of."

Cheryl thought about the proverb written on the back of the receipt. "The receipt. 'The time to make friends is before you need them.'" She looked at Mickey. "You wrote that on purpose, didn't you?"

He nodded. "I read it in a book somewhere, and it struck me as something to remember. I try to be a good friend, but I think sometimes I don't work as hard at it as I should. Since Wanda died, I've been living in a shell."

"Well we are your friends," Naomi said quietly. "You worked with Seth for a long time, and I know he considers you a friend. Why don't you come to our house for dinner one night next week?"

Mickey brightened. "Thank you. I'd be honored." He went to join Velma back in the house with the group.

"What will happen to them?" Naomi asked.

"I think they will be okay," Roy said. "My grandma only had wonderful things to say. That seems to be the consensus between the whole group. This might be one of those situations where it's best to just let it go."

"I think they've learned a lesson. Poor Mickey looks like he hasn't eaten in days," Naomi said. "I will speak to Seth and see if we can all have a work day here to help Velma and her husband. It looks like a lot got accomplished the past few days, and I think with a good day's work, they will be ready to sell."

Roy looked around at the barn. "It sure is a nice place."

Cheryl didn't miss the wistful expression on his face. "Don't tell me you'd be interested in it."

He shrugged. "It's not practical, but I've always wanted a nice piece of land and some animals. I grew up in the city, but my grandparents had a farm in Virginia when I was young. It would be a big change, but I'd certainly consider it." He grinned. "Cheryl, you have my card. If you'd e-mail me when the place comes on the market, I would appreciate it."

Lacey burst into the barn, her granny wig askew. "You're not going to believe this." She crossed her arms and scowled. "I mean, seriously. Not. Gonna. Believe. It." She emphasized each word.

"Probably not," Cheryl said. "But if you'd told me the events of the past four days a week ago, I wouldn't have believed that either. Now I know that causing tour buses full of people to disappear is something that can be rationalized if you're in enough trouble. So tell us."

"It's Blake. This time he's gone too far. Like here's the line"—Lacey drew a line in the dirt with her toe—"and he's way over there so far from the line that he can't even see it." She pointed to the far side of the barn where a cow was looking at them curiously.

"That bad?" Cheryl hadn't been impressed with anything Lacey had said about the man over the last few days, so she wasn't altogether shocked that he'd once again crossed the line.

"He made the whole stalker thing up. For publicity. He knew Michael wanted to get in touch with me about this reality series idea. But instead of just relaying the message, he told me that I might be in danger. Then he leaked it to the press. He's also the one who leaked my possible whereabouts while I was here." She took a breath. "Not to mention that he gave Michael my e-mail and phone number and had him send me messages over the past few days. The sole purpose was to keep me scared."

"That's crazy." Cheryl shook her head.

"Oh, it gets better. Blake and Michael are the ones who've been following me around. Blake says that for one, he wanted to keep an eye on me—and that I've been eating too much cheese. And he also wanted my fear to be authentic so that I'd be easier to manage."

"That's low," Roy growled. "Is he still out there? I'd like to have a word with him."

Lacey shook her head. "No way. I sent them both packing. Of course, Blake says he was only trying to keep me in the news. He wanted to be able to tell the media that someone had followed me here. And he needed me to believe it, so he kept me in the dark." She shook her head. "He thinks with a lot of drama and mystery surrounding me, it gives me more star power. So basically it's like life is his own chess game, and I'm a pawn. You know?" Lacey buried her head in her hands. "I always trusted him to help me make good business decisions and to take on the right projects. But clearly my trust was misplaced."

"I'm sorry." Cheryl couldn't imagine not being able to trust those closest to her. Lacey must feel very betrayed.

"I was scared for my life, always looking over my shoulder. When the media started talking about me being in Sugarcreek, I was so disappointed that I'd been found out. Turns out, it was my own manager who was behind the whole thing."

"How did you leave things with him?"

Lacey rubbed her eyes. "There was really only one thing I could do. I fired him. I pay good money to him, and in return I expect honesty. I expect to have someone in that position who is looking out for my best interests—not trying to stir up drama and keep me splashed on magazine covers." She sighed. "He threatened for breach of contract, but I let him know that I wouldn't mind telling the world what he'd done—and I have witnesses. No one would ever hire him again if they knew how he'd treated me."

"Good for you," Roy said, a look of admiration on his face.

Lacey smiled. "I want to be taken seriously. But thanks to Blake, I think most people just think I'm one of those Hollywood party girls who thrive on drama. I want to become a respected actress. I want to continue writing and performing my own songs."

"That sounds very reasonable." Cheryl was happy for her friend. She was actually going to miss having Lacey around.

"Plus, I really want to be very deliberate in the projects I choose and even the events I attend. This weekend has made me stop and consider what's really important. I don't want to continue to keep my faith a secret. I want people to know that God has blessed me and that He is the one I want to be sure I please—not a crowd or a critic. I tried to discuss that with Blake just now, and instead of embracing it, he pushed back, saying I might be limiting myself in Hollywood if I go that route."

"Do you think that's true?" Roy asked.

"Maybe," Lacey admitted. "But you know, if finally standing up for what I believe means certain roles don't come my way, then I don't think they are roles I'd want anyway."

Cheryl had to admit she was impressed. "It sounds like you've really done some thinking while you've been here."

"Watching the people around here—the way they live their lives to serve God—it's an amazing thing to see. And going to church with you this morning showed me how much I miss it. The verse about how God has a plan for us that the pastor referenced, it really spoke to me and made me consider how I'm spending the years that I have."

"I am glad your time here has been beneficial. Even though you did not get to take part in the tour as you had planned, perhaps you still came away with something worth your time," Naomi said.

Lacey grinned. "Oh, definitely. And plus I met you and Cheryl." She gestured at Cheryl.

"And?" Roy teased. "What about me?"

"Okay, and you too." Lacey's face flushed with happiness. "Plus I finally learned what a scuz Blake is."

"Not to mention helping to find a whole busload of lost people. Even though they had no idea they were lost." Cheryl shook her head. "What a weekend we've had."

Chapter Twenty-Six

Monday morning dawned bright and clear. Although Cheryl woke up relieved that the mystery of the disappearing tour group had been solved, she was also a little sad. The past few days had been so full and exciting. Between Lacey crashing at her house, Roy popping in with news, Kathy consulting with her about Michael, not to mention searching high and low for the bus... the usual January blues had gone away. Cheryl had always thought of those weeks after Christmas as a little gloomy after the holidays, but that feeling had definitely been replaced this year.

Cheryl quickly got ready for work and made her way to the kitchen. "You all packed?" she asked as Lacey joined her at the table.

"Sure am." She grinned. "It's kinda nice to be back in my own clothes." The oversized blue sweater she had on just matched her eyes. Paired with skinny jeans and brown riding boots, she was a far cry from the costumes of the previous days. "Roy isn't going to know what to think. He's never seen me dressed as me."

"I imagine he'll be pleased."

Lacey giggled. "It was actually kind of nice to get to know him while I was in costumes. I mean, old lady Lacey and Amish Lacey caught his eye. I think that means he wasn't interested in me just for my looks."

"Did you stay up late last again night talking to him on the phone?"

"Yeah." She ran her fingers through her long dark brown hair. "He says he's coming by the store first thing this morning. He has news about Riggins and McGraw."

"Good. I like all the loose ends tied up. I was wondering if we'd learn why they were after Ethyl." Cheryl scooped Beau up in her arms. "Now that things are back to normal, I think Beau should go with us to the store today."

Fifteen minutes later, they arrived at the Swiss Miss. "I'm going to be sad to leave this place," Lacey said. "I'll definitely come back for a visit." She took Beau while Cheryl unlocked the door. "I mean if that's okay with you."

Cheryl laughed. "Of course. It's been lots of fun to have you here. You'll have to come back when it's not so cold. The place is really gorgeous in the fall." She flipped on the lights.

"Thanks. I guess I kind of invited myself to be your houseguest for the weekend. I really am thankful you let me stay."

"Don't mention it."

"And hey, if you ever want to come out to LA, I'll totally let you crash at my place."

Cheryl had Googled just to see what kind of place Lacey was used to living in. She was certain that she and Beau could stay in a wing of Lacey's mansion and Lacey would never even know they were there. "Thanks. I just might take you up on that someday." Traveling to LA might need to go on her bucket list. And who knew? Maybe Lacey could get her to a red carpet or a premiere or something.

The bell above the door jingled, and Roy walked in grinning broadly. "Good morning, ladies." He held up two coffees from Wallhouse. "Two mochas. I took a chance that you both liked chocolate." He smiled. "And coffee."

Cheryl and Lacey both took one.

"Yes and yes," said Cheryl. "Thank you."

Lacey nodded. "Me too. That was very thoughtful."

"I wanted to fill you in on McGraw and Riggins and my grandma. It's actually kind of an interesting story and definitely the case of someone being in the wrong place at the wrong time."

Cheryl motioned for them to follow her to the back room so they could sit down.

Once they were seated, Roy continued. "Thursday was a sunny day and warmer than normal. Grandma decided to go to the park to walk a lap before her book-club meeting. While she was there, she got a drink in the water fountain. While she was drinking, she saw a man—McGraw—put a lipstick tube down beneath a park bench. He walked off and left it."

"Which explains why they wanted me to give them my lipstick." Lacey shook her head. "I totally tried to give them one in every shade." She giggled. "They must've thought I was crazy."

Roy nodded. "Anyway, Grandma went over and picked it up. She thought it might be something bad. She said maybe some kind of drugs or a knife or something. She knew there was no reason a burly man like McGraw would be putting out that lipstick in a public place unless he was up to no good."

"Smart lady," Cheryl said.

"What Grandma didn't know was that Riggins was waiting in the wings to pick up the delivery. When she picked it up instead, he first thought he'd been duped."

"She really was in the wrong place at the wrong time," Lacey said. "And bless her heart, it sounds like she was only trying to do a good deed."

Roy nodded in agreement. "She was. She was afraid a little kid would pick it up and get hurt." He shook his head. "Anyway, she stuck it in her purse and headed to her car. She said last night that she didn't know why she didn't just throw it away, but she was just thinking she'd toss it out when she got home."

"And I'll bet that's when the car chase began." Cheryl took a sip of her coffee.

"Sure was. You ladies know the rest."

"Wait," Lacey said. "We know what happened, but we don't know why. What was so special about that lipstick tube?"

"Well, I'm not going to give any names here because it's definitely someone you've both heard of... but that lipstick tube is actually a jump drive. It had some pretty incriminating information about an individual who is one of the leading presidential candidates. McGraw works for the person who had the information, and Riggins works for the candidate. McGraw was dropping the evidence off in exchange for a wire transfer."

"So we were kinda right," Cheryl said. "We thought Riggins and McGraw weren't very good partners. It's because they're not. In fact, it sounds like they work for people who may not get along very well."

"Exactly. The only thing Riggins and McGraw have in common is that they both have powerful bosses, and they knew losing that jump drive wasn't an option. That's why they chased after Grandma. They just wanted it back."

"Wow. I'm so glad she ran in here when she did," Cheryl said. "They seemed like they would've done just about anything to get what they wanted."

"We are all very blessed that things turned out as well as they did," Roy agreed.

Cheryl stood. She'd give Lacey and Roy some time alone before the bus got to the store. She excused herself and went out front. Esther wouldn't be in until the afternoon, which gave Cheryl time to take care of some much-needed inventory. It would be Valentine's Day before long, and Cheryl had a few special items she needed to have in stock. Candy for sure. Maybe some neat gift items as well.

The bell dinged as Mickey held open the door for the group. Cheryl was overwhelmed by their positive comments. She planned to e-mail a survey to the group later and get their feedback on the tour, but from the comments she heard, it sounded like most would be good ones.

She rang up a number of purchases as many customers, including Roy's grandma, decided to purchase souvenirs from the Swiss Miss.

"Thanks, Mrs. Ethyl," she said as she rang up a jar of apple butter. "I think you'll enjoy this when you get home."

"Oh yes, I will." She smiled. "I see Roy has found himself a pretty girl to talk to." She motioned toward Lacey and Roy where they stood picking out Amish dolls. "He's got so much to offer. It's nice to see him so happy." She beamed.

"Are you headed back home today?" Cheryl asked.

Ethyl nodded. "I sure am. I can't wait to get home. It was sort of an unexpected vacation for me."

"Roy filled me in. I'm glad you're safe."

"Thanks. I'll see you again soon. I'm definitely coming back." Ethyl collected her package and made her way over to where Roy and Lacey were standing.

Before long, it was time for the group to leave for the airport, and things reached a fever pitch. Cheryl rang up several purchases in a row as tour goers tried to get their last-minute shopping done and get back on the bus. "Thanks so much," she said as she rang up the last customer in line.

Cheryl hurried out the door just in time to see the bus door close, and the bus slowly began its departure from Sugarcreek. She waved at the group, realizing she'd never gotten the chance to say good-bye to Lacey.

Maybe giving Esther the morning off hadn't been such a great idea. She should've known they'd be swamped.

The store was quiet and empty when she stepped back inside. Back to normal.

Cheryl went about her business, cleaning and organizing. She planned out the Valentine's Day display and tried not to think about being alone on a day set aside to celebrate couples.

The bell over the door jingled, and Lacey burst through the door, followed by Roy.

"Did I miss the bus?" she asked then burst out laughing. "I'm kidding." She smiled and held up her phone. "Actually we were taking a picture by that cuckoo clock."

"Why am I not surprised?"

"It's the first in a series of photos we're going to take—all the roadside attractions between here and Alabama," Roy explained.

Cheryl widened her eyes and looked at Lacey. "You're going home?"

Lacey nodded. "Roy offered to drive me. It only takes about ten hours from here." She smiled broadly. "I can't wait to surprise my mom." She smiled. "It will be just like my TV movie, *The Art of Surprise*. Only way better." She giggled.

"Now that Grandma is safe and sound, I think I could use a little time off. I cut my vacation short to get here this weekend after all." Roy grinned. "And Cheryl, thanks for your assistance with cracking the case. I doubt you'll get such a thanks from Chief Twitchell, but I assure you, we all appreciate it."

"You're welcome."

He gave her a stern look. "But in the future, try not to get in the middle of a potential shoot-out. The two of you should have waited in the car until I arrived."

Cheryl nodded. She didn't point out that Lacey's granny disguise and a dimly lit barn worked together to draw McGraw and Riggins out. "If we'd ever thought we were in real danger, we certainly wouldn't have gotten out of the car."

"I'm glad to hear it." Roy put an arm around Lacey's shoulders.

"Once we've visited my mom and her family in Alabama, we'll drive back here. I'll stay with Nana and Papa until time for the movie to shoot."

"I know you'll be relieved to finally spend some time with your family."

"I've already cancelled the first leg of the world tour. It was all booked too tightly. The truth is, I'm afraid of burnout. Being here for a few days and slowing down some has shown me that I need to take time off every now and then to rejuvenate."

"Keep me posted on that tour. I think you'll have some fans from Sugarcreek who'll want to attend the nearest show."

Lacey grinned. "I'd love that. And hey—when I'm in Dover, we'll have to hang out. I'd love to have dinner at that amazing buffet again."

"Sounds like a plan." Cheryl watched the interaction between Lacey and Roy. Something about the combo seemed to work. She hoped they would find happiness with each other.

Lacey bought a sack full of Amish dolls and homemade jam. "I'll be back soon," she said. "And please keep in touch." She handed Cheryl a slip of paper. "It's my number. To my *main* phone. You'd better use it."

"I will," Cheryl promised.

Lacey hugged her good-bye then gave Beau a scratch behind the ears. "Bye, buddy."

Cheryl wished both Lacey and Roy well and watched them walk out the door, hand in hand.

It was apparent that Lacey had learned a few lessons during her time among the plain people in Sugarcreek. And maybe Cheryl had come away with a few lessons of her own.

Part of Velma's motivation for doing what she'd done was that she didn't have any close friends whom she could call upon during her time of need. Watching Velma struggle as she admitted how she needed help had really made Cheryl consider her own situation. She may not be in a dating relationship, but she had formed some close friendships since she came to Sugarcreek. Maybe for now, that was enough.

The bell above the door jingled.

Kathy and Heather walked in.

"I hear you have a few bits of news we might be interested in," Kathy said.

"Boy do I have a story." She filled them in on the events of the previous night, including Michael's and Blake's devious actions.

"I'd pretty much decided he was up to no good," Heather said. "I just couldn't quite figure out what he was up to."

Cheryl had gotten the rest of Michael's story from Lacey after they got home last night. "He was quizzing you because he needed an insider with knowledge about the Amish and the area. It helped that he also thought you were cute."

Heather blushed.

"His goal was to develop a reality show set here in Sugarcreek, but the reality is that there wouldn't have been much truth to it. I'm guessing he eventually would've asked you to pretend to be

Amish. No one that he approached was interested in participating. He was hoping Lacey would throw her star power behind him and help him out, but she never would've done that—not even if he'd approached her through the right channels."

"It seems like there've been all sorts of interesting things going on these past few days," Kathy remarked. "Heather told me she even saw a guest at Silo Church yesterday, and you'll never guess who it was."

Cheryl hoped she knew the answer. "Who?"

"Richard Wellaby. Doesn't that just beat all? As far as I know, that man hasn't had one nice thing to say about any of our local churches."

"He was there all right. I got there a bit late and had to sit in the back. Richard was already seated in the same row. He even nodded at me when I smiled at him."

Cheryl would have to be sure to let Aunt Mitzi know. Maybe Lacey was right—maybe being a missionary in your own community was important. "That's great. Maybe we won't have Mean Richard to contend with much longer. Maybe soon he'll just be Richard." She couldn't help but think of Richard's story and how unrequited love had turned him into such a bitter man. Perhaps the love that could be found at Silo Church could help him get past some of those old wounds and give him hope for the future.

"That would be a welcome change." Kathy smiled. She motioned toward the door. "We'd better get back to the Honey Bee. The lunch crowd will be in shortly."

Cheryl told them good-bye and returned to her inventory. She was relieved that Heather was taking the news about Michael's real intentions so well. Sometimes those who appeared to be the weakest were quite strong when tested. She suspected Heather would be just fine and would find a man of honor. She said a quick prayer of thanks to God for all He'd done in Sugarcreek this weekend.

Chapter Twenty-Seven

It had been a slow Monday afternoon, but Cheryl had enjoyed the lull. She'd neglected so much over the past week as she prepared for the tour and then got lost in the frenzy of the long weekend. It was nice to catch up on bookkeeping and inventory, not to mention sending out the post-tour surveys.

Just before it was time to display the Closed sign, Levi Miller stepped in the Swiss Miss and smiled. "Goot afternoon, Cheryl."

She returned his smile. "You missed seeing the tour group off. They should already be at the airport by now—in fact many of them should already be in the air." She smoothed her hair. "Except for Lacey. She and Roy are driving to Alabama to see her family."

"Sounds like fun. I enjoyed spending time with them Saturday night." He held up a bag. "I brought some jam and bread. Esther told us the stock was running low again." He eyed the shelf it usually sat on. "From the looks of it, she was right."

"We had kind of a rush today with the group leaving and all. It seems like Velma served a lot of Naomi's bread and jam, and they were hooked on it."

He chuckled. "I don't blame them."

"And I ate the last bit of my own personal stock a couple days ago." She grinned. "I know what I'll be eating for supper tonight."

Levi returned her grin, then his gaze turned serious. "I did come to bring you some merchandise, but I also came to see how you were doing. I know the weekend was stressful for you."

Tears flooded her eyes, and she blinked them away. Levi would no doubt think her to be nuts if he saw them. But the fact that he cared enough to come check on her made her feel so good. And to be honest with herself, it made her heart flutter a little bit too. Even though their relationship had a definite mark of uncertainty about it, she knew one thing: his was one of the friendships she could count on. She thought about the conversation she'd had with Lacey. The qualities she'd listed that would make Levi a good boyfriend also made him a good friend. And that was a blessing.

"Stressful, yes. It was also a little exciting and kind of fun." She grinned. "Last night things were a little tense for a bit."

"Naomi told us. I'm impressed that you figured out Velma was involved based on some lotion."

Cheryl laughed. "Well, it was sunless tanning lotion. You know—the stuff that makes you look like you have a tan even in the winter and even if you've not been in the sunshine."

Levi wrinkled his nose. "I can honestly say that is nothing I have ever used." He grinned. "Or ever plan to use."

"Good call. I know it's a little weird, but I noticed the first time Velma came into the store that she was kind of orange tinted. That's a side effect of that kind of lotion, especially for some skin tones. So when I saw the bottle of lotion in the bag Lacey had accidentally picked up, I was pretty sure I knew who was behind the whole thing."

"It is too bad they did not just ask for help. Daed and I discussed it this morning. We would have pitched in and helped if we had only known."

"Sometimes people don't like to ask for help. In Velma's case, she didn't feel like they had friends to help them other than Mickey. And they needed a lot more manpower than just him."

"We are planning a work day there tomorrow. We'll see what needs to be done and try to help her get it ready to sell."

Cheryl remembered Roy's request that she contact him if it went up for sale. At first she'd thought he was just saying that, but after seeing him and Lacey this morning, it wouldn't surprise her at all for the two of them to end up together and have a residence in Hollywood and a farm near Sugarcreek. "I'm just very thankful everyone was safe and came away with a good experience. From the buzz of the group today, I'd say we're going to get rave reviews on our little joint business venture." She smiled.

Levi smiled back at her. "So does that mean you are ready to start planning a spring tour?"

Cheryl laughed. "For now...no. But in the future, you never know."

And that was the great thing about the future. It really was wide open with possibilities. The possibility that they'd offer another tour. The possibility that they'd take their friendship to a new level. Yes, her future in Sugarcreek was full of hope.

And in Cheryl's book, that meant her life was headed in the right direction. Her own life, just like the tour bus—just like Lacey and Roy's road trip—had gone off the path she'd expected it to. Even so, things had turned out better than she ever could have planned.

And just like Aunt Mitzi had reminded her in her recent letter, it didn't matter how many plans she made—God's purpose for her life was what mattered.

Author Letter

Dear Reader,

The first time I visited Sugarcreek was in 2009. I had a book-signing in nearby Charm, Ohio, which was the setting of my very first book. I knew then that there was something special about Sugarcreek. Years later when that book was made into a TV movie, the studio chose Sugarcreek as the filming location.

I was thrilled to get to return to the quaint town and discover some new favorite places as well as visit some of the spots I visited on my first trip. The people of Sugarcreek were so welcoming, and the scenery is beautiful. (Not to mention the food…it's pretty amazing too!)

It's been so fun getting to revisit Sugarcreek with this series. I adore cozy mysteries, so getting to write one against the backdrop of Sugarcreek has been a real treat.

Thanks so much for reading!

Blessings,
Annalisa Daughety

About the Author

Annalisa Daughety is the best-selling author of more than fifteen novels and novellas including the Walk in the Park series, *Love Finds You in Charm, Ohio*, and *A Wedding to Remember in Charleston*. She writes contemporary stories set in historic locations and classifies her writing style as romantic comedy.

Annalisa lives in Arkansas with her husband, Johnny, and when she's not working or writing, she enjoys raising chickens, gardening, and traveling. She loves connecting with readers on Facebook, Twitter, Instagram, and Pinterest. Find more information about Annalisa at www.annalisadaughety.com.

Fun Fact about the Amish or Sugarcreek, Ohio

Sometimes I think it surprises people that a girl from small-town Arkansas and no ties to the Amish community writes Amish fiction. I admit, I'm still learning about the Amish and their beliefs and customs—and thankfully I've had some wonderful editors who've helped steer me in the right direction as I research. One of the interesting things that I've learned in my journey of writing Amish fiction is that Amish men don't wear wedding rings. Instead, they stop shaving their beards the day they get married, and their beard signifies that they are married. They continue to shave their mustaches, but their beards grow longer with each passing year of marriage.

Something Delicious from Our Sugarcreek Friends

Amish Fry Pie

2 cups all-purpose flour
½ teaspoon salt
1 teaspoon baking powder
1 tablespoon sugar
6 tablespoons cold butter
1 egg yolk
⅓ cup milk
1 egg white
2 cups pie filling of your choice

Shortening or oil for frying
2 tablespoons melted butter
2 tablespoons milk
1 teaspoon vanilla extract
2 cups powdered sugar (adjust the amount of powdered sugar to the desired thickness of glaze)

Mix flour, salt, baking powder, and sugar, then cut in cold butter using two knives, a pastry blender, or food processor.

Beat the egg yolk into the milk, then gently mix it in to form a dough—knead as little as possible.

Divide the dough into eight to nine small balls. Roll them out into four- to five-inch circles.

Spread about one-quarter cup of pie filling on each circle. Moisten the edges with egg white, then seal with a fry-pie press or fold in half and seal with the tines of a fork.

Heat shortening or oil in a skillet to about 375 degrees. Deep fry pies for about two minutes per side, until golden brown. Fry two to three pies at a time to avoid crowding the pan.

Remove pies to a cooling rack while you fry the remaining pies. Watch that the oil does not get too hot, or the pies will brown too quickly.

Mix the melted butter, milk, vanilla, and powdered sugar to form a glaze. The glaze should be runny but with enough thickness to allow it to set up as it cools. (You may need to adjust the powdered sugar and/or milk to achieve the right consistency.) Drizzle the glaze over the slightly cooled fry pies.

Serve warm or store in an air-tight container.

Read on for a sneak peek of another exciting book in the series Sugarcreek Amish Mysteries!

Peace Like a River
by Olivia Newport

How her aunt Mitzi knew she was drooling over the cashmere-lined, hand-stitched soft leather gloves in the Bloomingdale's catalog remained a mystery to Cheryl Cooper. But she should not have been surprised when she discovered the boxed gloves on a pantry shelf with one of her aunt's yellow envelopes taped to the gray paisley wrapping paper and Cheryl's name underscored with three curvy lines.

Still treating the gloves with admiration, Cheryl folded them carefully and assured herself they were secure in her jacket pockets. Since making a rapid decision a few months ago to move from Columbus and accept Aunt Mitzi's invitation to manage both her home and her quaint gifts and sundries shop in Sugarcreek, Ohio, Cheryl found at least one letter or gift every few weeks tucked away in an obscure spot. Last month it was the gloves, and Cheryl had taken to wearing them during her late afternoon walks on the path running along the river on one end of the town. On some days it seemed silly to drive to a location just to get out to walk. Why not just walk there in the first place? But at this time of year,

Cheryl fought the fading light if she wanted to get in a brisk constitutional after closing up the Swiss Miss and before settling in at home with a book, her supper, and her cat.

The note with the gloves had said simply,

> When you warm up your fingers, know how much the thought of you warms my heart, no matter how many miles separate us.
>
> Love,
> Aunt Mitzi

For a mid-February Monday, the day was uncharacteristically warm even as the afternoon waned and genuine evening approached. As Cheryl loosened the sky-blue scarf swaddling her neck at the top of her burgundy jacket, she reached the highest point along the route she now took four or five times a week. From here she could look in one direction toward the orange orb sliding behind the rising evening shadows and in the other direction toward the festive lights of Sugarcreek. Some flickered off as businesses closed for the day, but others outlined store windows inviting visitors to enjoy the town's charm at any time of day.

How normal it all seemed now.

Only a few months ago, Aunt Mitzi's offer came out of the blue. *Come to Sugarcreek. Run my store. Live in my home. Free me to be a missionary in Papua New Guinea as I've always wanted.*

And what was there to keep Cheryl in Columbus? A job she'd lost interest in. A broken five-year engagement to a man for whom she'd waited far too long before realizing Lance would never be ready for marriage. Cheryl had friends and a church she enjoyed, but she preferred to believe thirty was not too old to build a new life somewhere different. That's what Mitzi was doing, and she was twice as old as Cheryl. Mitzi deserved to chase the dream of her youth. She and Ralph were married for forty happy years. Throughout her childhood and young adulthood, Cheryl saw this for herself. But Uncle Ralph had passed away several years ago. Mitzi was on her own. Why should she not answer the call to missions that was as unambiguous now as it had been before she married? "Sixty is the new forty," Aunt Mitzi always said. She was in excellent health and a keen learner. Cheryl was delighted to launch her aunt's pursuit with the confidence that the Swiss Miss would be well minded in her absence, no matter how long Mitzi might be gone.

The agreement papers were signed, permissions authorized, Sugarcreek introductions made. Now instead of being chummy with the other assistant branch manager of the bank where she used to work, Cheryl's favorite companion was Naomi Miller. If anyone at the bank in Columbus had told her she would feel this attached to a farmer's wife ten years her senior wearing the plain dress and bonnet of the Amish, Cheryl would have laughed. Now Cheryl looked forward to the days each week Naomi turned up at the Swiss Miss with breads and jams and sweet treats that sold faster than Cheryl could log them into inventory. Even more, though, Cheryl hoped Naomi would have time for a cup of tea and a quiet chat when she came in. Since arriving in Sugarcreek, Cheryl savored the small bits of her day that brought her pleasure—and they were bountiful.

For instance, for the first time in her adult life, Cheryl had time to walk along a riverbank, breathe deeply, and let peace lap against her spirit. She was hard-pressed to think what could make her want to give up this newfound habit. Even on frigid days, when most of the town looked forward to huddling beside their fireplaces, Cheryl anticipated her walks with enthusiasm.

Exhaling, Cheryl lowered the zipper on her jacket by four inches. This was the warmest day she remembered since before Thanksgiving, and the brisk mile and a half she had just power walked helped disperse heat beneath her layers.

The river was a tributary of some sort of the Tuscawaras River, eventually tracing back to the Mississippi. Its movement had slowed after Christmas and through the weeks of January, but the temperatures had climbed steadily the last few days, and the sun was winter bright. Several times as she walked, Cheryl heard the crack of splitting ice on the frozen surface and the escaping rush of the water gathering speed below.

Cheryl's gaze shifted from the setting sun to the slope of the stony riverbank about forty yards ahead.

Something looked unusual.

Trailing along the bank was a ragged path of oddball items. From this distance and in the shifting light, Cheryl wasn't sure what she saw—but she was certain it was more than the normal rocks, soggy soil, and patches of ice. She dipped her head forward to peer with more intention, but all she could make out was that the clutter looked as if someone had dumped a trash bin or the contents of an abandoned garage. There didn't seem to be a pattern to the shapes and sizes of what she saw, but her heart sank at the sight of the mess that would only get worse overnight.

She jumped at the sound of steps behind her and immediately chastised herself. Anyone could walk along the river, of course, and she thought she had broken the habit of city fears. In Columbus, Lance constantly thought he should prepare for every bad thing that might happen, and Cheryl had absorbed his caution. After she moved to Sugarcreek, she embraced the notion that there was a difference between sensible circumspection, which she believed she practiced, and living under irrational fear, which she refused to continue doing. Life was too short to always be afraid.

But she admitted relief that the brisk footfalls she heard belonged to Rueben Vogel and not a stranger.

"Rueben!" Cheryl said. "What are you doing out here?"

"Same as you, I imagine," Rueben said. "Walking. Enjoying the river. Watching for the first star."

Watching for the first star. Cheryl liked that thought.

"I haven't seen you out here before," she said, "at least not at this time of day."

"It is a new habit." Rueben's blue eyes twinkled. "I may be an old man, but I am not dead yet. Any time I try to help around the farm, my daughter and her husband shoo me off. A body can only spend so much time rocking in a *dawdy haus*."

Cheryl laughed. "I always wondered what you did when you weren't playing checkers with your brother in my aunt's store."

"The farm is not far from here," Rueben said. "Perhaps a mile. No reason I shouldn't get out and about."

Cheryl pointed a thumb in the direction of the scattered trash. "Any idea what happened down there?"

Rueben twisted his head back in the direction he'd come from. "I'd better head back if I want to get home before my daughter calls me for supper and discovers I am gone."

"I've met your daughter," Cheryl said, teasing. "She's hardly a jailer."

He put a finger to his lips. "*Shh.* If the trees can clap their hands to praise God, they may also have ears."

Cheryl laughed again as Rueben pivoted his wiry frame and set a tenacious pace. Only after he was out of earshot did Cheryl realize he hadn't answered her question—did he know anything about the motley mess farther down the river? She was certain it had not been there yesterday, on Sunday afternoon, when she walked in full daylight. It could have been there as long as twenty-four hours or as briefly as one. She glanced in the direction she had left her car, calculating that she could walk a few more yards before heading home for her own supper.

When she looked again at the strewn debris, she saw another man. He hadn't been there five minutes ago—at least he had not been within view from Cheryl's location.

But there he was. An Amish man in his telltale black trousers, jacket, and hat.

Cheryl couldn't make out who he was. Certainly she didn't know all the Amish men around Sugarcreek by name. She crept forward, watching. The wind kicked up, beginning to bite.

At first Cheryl thought the scattered items must belong to the man or he was responsible for them in some way. Why else would he be picking through the hodgepodge with as much deliberation as he exhibited? Perhaps a tub tumbled out of a buggy on the road above the river. Maybe he was transporting a load as a favor for an *Englisch* neighbor. Or he might have a salvage business and had picked up a load. Any number of explanations might suit the circumstances. Cheryl felt sorry for the man. Restoring order to the wreckage was a most unpleasant close to the day. If she helped him, it would go faster. Clearing the shambles that marred the view would not have been entirely disagreeable if they at least had trash bags or boxes. Cheryl quickened her pace and then slowed in fresh realization.

The man was not trying to restore order. He picked up one item after another only to cast it aside without serious inspection. Cheryl couldn't tell what most of them were. Small shapes in the shadows from the distance were difficult to distinguish. He was interested in one particular piece of the debris.

Cheryl watched, haunted by a sense that she ought to know who this man was. The temperature was falling along with the light. Cheryl rezipped her jacket against the wind.

The man untangled a rope or a small hose—Cheryl was not sure which—and extracted the item he had been fixated on all along. He held it in one hand and ran the fingers of his other hand along its length horizontally before turning it to stand on end. It was some sort of a thick stick with painted worn stripes. Only when the man flipped it in the other direction and Cheryl saw the broad flat end now turned up in the air did she realize it was an old oar.

And the man's stature, now that she'd had time to study it, looked like Seth Miller.

Cheryl cupped her mouth and called out. "Seth!"

But the wind threw her effort back into her own face, and the man made no response. Instead, he kicked his work boots free of the nearest items, gripped the oar, and began walking in the opposite direction.

Meet the Real People of Sugarcreek

Sprinkled amid our created characters in Sugarcreek Amish Mysteries, we've fictionally depicted some of the town's real-life people and businesses. Here's a glimpse into the actual story of Sugarcreek Village Inn.

Have you ever wanted to sleep in a train car? You can do just that if you visit the Sugarcreek Village Inn. Located in the heart of Sugarcreek's Swiss Village and just a block from Main Street, the Sugarcreek Village Inn hosts two vintage train cars that have been turned into delightful accommodations.

It's a real treat for young and old alike to spend a night or two in one of the vintage train cars. They're even stationed on their own train track! Of course, if sleeping in a train car isn't for you, the inn is right next door and is just as quaint.

A Note from the Editors

We hope you enjoy Sugarcreek Amish Mysteries, created by the Books and Inspirational Media Division of Guideposts, a nonprofit organization that touches millions of lives every day through products and services that inspire, encourage, help you grow in your faith, and celebrate God's love in every aspect of your daily life.

Thank you for making a difference with your purchase of this book, which helps fund our many outreach programs to military personnel, prisons, hospitals, nursing homes, and educational institutions. To learn more, visit GuidepostsFoundation.org.

We also maintain many useful and uplifting online resources. Visit Guideposts.org to read true stories of hope and inspiration, access OurPrayer network, sign up for free newsletters, download free e-books, join our Facebook community, and follow our stimulating blogs.

To learn about other Guideposts publications, including the best-selling devotional *Daily Guideposts*, go to ShopGuideposts.org, call (800) 932-2145, or write to Guideposts, PO Box 5815, Harlan, Iowa 51593.

Sign up for the Guideposts Fiction Newsletter

and stay up-to-date on the fiction you love!

You'll get sneak peeks of new releases, recommendations from other Guideposts readers, and special offers just for you...

And it's FREE!

Just go to Guideposts.org/newsletters today to sign up.

Visit ShopGuideposts.org or call (800) 932-2145

Find more inspiring fiction in these best-loved Guideposts series

Secrets of the Blue Hill Library
Enjoy the tingle of suspense and the joy of coming home when Anne Gibson turns her late aunt's Victorian mansion into a library and uncovers hidden secrets.

Miracles of Marble Cove
Follow four women who are drawn together to face life's challenges, support one another in faith, and experience God's amazing grace as they encounter mysterious events in the small town of Marble Cove.

Secrets of Mary's Bookshop
Delve into a cozy mystery where Mary, the owner of Mary's Mystery Bookshop, finds herself using sleuthing skills that she didn't realize she had. There are quirky characters and lots of unexpected twists and turns.

Patchwork Mysteries
Discover that life's little mysteries often have a common thread in a series where every novel contains an intriguing mystery centered around a quilt located in a beautiful New England town.

Mysteries of Silver Peak
Escape to the historic mining town of Silver Peak, Colorado, and discover how one woman's love of antiques helps her solve mysteries buried deep in the town's checkered past.

**To learn more about these books,
visit ShopGuideposts.org**